Second Chance With You

BAXTER BOYS
BOOK FOUR

JESSIE GUSSMAN

Contents

Acknowledgments

Cover art by Julia Gussman
Editing by Heather Hayden
Narration by Jay Dyess
Author Services by CE Author Assistant

~

Listen to the unabridged audio for FREE performed by Jay Dyess on the Say with Jay channel on YouTube. Get early access to all of Jay's recordings and listen to Jessie's books before they're available to the general public, plus get daily Bible readings by Jay and bonus scenes by becoming a Say with Jay channel member.

Chapter One

Riley Coleman's phone buzzed. She kept her hands folded in her lap and didn't move.

"That terminal is sitting at the confluence of the turnpike, 180, and 199, right in the middle of central Pennsylvania. We're perfectly positioned to be everywhere and go anywhere." Her dad's booming voice filled the corner office of Coleman Trucking and Repair, Inc., in Spruce Mountain, Maine.

Her phone stopped buzzing. Riley didn't twitch.

"It should be our top performing shop. It should be number one in the country. We have state-of-the-art computer systems and mechanics from the top schools anywhere." His face brightened like the red of her mother's old countertops. "But it's not. It's the worst-performing diesel garage we own. The bottom in just about every measurable area."

Their company had a trucking division and a repair division with a fleet of two hundred trucks and ten repair terminals scattered over the country. The location they were currently at was the original one.

Her dad stood up, tall, as always, with a slightly larger waistline than when Riley had last seen him at Christmastime. "It's not just because you're my daughter. It's because you've made this shop, in

Nowheretown, Maine, the best-performing shop in the country. The job in Pennsylvania is yours by rights."

Riley rose as well. Only his old office desk, ponderous and glowering, stood between them. "I can do the job." Her voice sounded capable and bold. A direct contrast to the timorous skittering of her heart.

"Bold as brass. That's what you've always been." Her dad smiled, a pleased I'm-proud-of-my-daughter smile. The kind she lived for.

She gave him a cool, confident smile in return. The smile she'd perfected over the years of demanding confrontations when her father insisted on and expected almost superhuman effort from her. But everything she'd worked for was almost within reach: make the shop in Pennsylvania successful, get the corner office, see her dad's approval.

"I need you down in Brickley Springs in three weeks, tops."

"I'll be there," she said, her confident tone covering her chaotic thoughts. Less than twenty-one days to wrap things up at the shop in Maine, move out of her apartment, and find somewhere to live. *No problem, Dad*.

He nodded, pacing behind his desk. His boots made a soft clomp on the tile floor. Outside the large windows, the late Maine spring was just turning the grass at the edge of the big truck parking area a happy shade of green. A direct contrast to the dark paneling and neutral colors of what used to be his office. Until ten years ago when he expanded his company and moved with his family to Pennsylvania.

Riley had grown up in Maine and had only left for college. She'd worked in the company all her life, working her way through college at the shop in Pennsylvania before coming back to Maine six years ago. She'd become the manager four years ago.

The same time Ben Baxter had been made shop foreman.

Riley's control slipped, and she pulled both lips between her teeth before she forced the tension out of her body and smoothed the features of her face. She wasn't going to think about Ben Baxter.

Except, if she wanted the shop in Pennsylvania to be successful, she didn't have a choice. Not only would she have to think about him, she'd have to convince him to move to Brickley Springs.

~

BEN BAXTER SET the last injector carefully on the plyboard and sawhorse makeshift table. He pulled the blue rag out of the back of his pocket and started wiping his hands, looking around at the almost deserted shop.

"Hey, boss. I'm leaving." Fred Tomlin, his gray hair sticking out from under his ball cap in wispy strands, stopped beside the gutted Peterbilt Ben had been working on.

"Thanks for staying and giving me a hand with that core." Ben shoved the rag back in his pocket.

"You still have a meeting with the fancy lady?" Fred asked with a smirk.

Riley Coleman wasn't hated around the shop. She was a fair manager and nice to look at, but with her business suits and perfectly shiny hair and nails, she would never be on their level. Which made her an outsider. Ben never bothered defending her. Not after what she'd done to him.

"Yep." Ben wiped the last of his wrenches off and set it back neatly in the drawer with the rest of the set. "She should be here any minute."

Fred paused in the act of raising his hat and rubbing his mostly bald head. "She's coming here?" he asked incredulously, hooking a finger in the pocket of his jeans. Most shops had a uniform policy. Ben had done away with it first thing when he'd become foreman. That wasn't the only change he made, but by the time the higher-ups realized what was going on, they couldn't argue with his improved output numbers. *Riley* couldn't argue. This wasn't their first meeting.

"Said she was." Ben carefully wiped off his three-quarter-inch socket.

This was their first meeting, however, in the shop. Every other time he'd been called on the carpet, he'd had to stand like a bad little schoolboy hanging his head in front of the principal's office. Never again. His sisters had graduated from high school and had several years of additional training under their belts. He could finally afford to take the risk he'd always wanted to take.

Fred's eyes swept over him, taking in the grease on his t-shirt, arms, and face. It mixed with the blood he'd wiped there when his forearm had clipped a jagged piece of metal after cutting off a stubborn bolt.

"Ain't you gonna clean up at all?"

"Nope." He gave Fred a grin. "Won't hurt the woman to see what a working man looks like."

Fred returned his grin and shrugged before turning. "See ya tomorrow."

"Flip the lights out for bays one and two before you go."

Fred didn't answer, just hit the switches on the way out the door.

Maybe he should have cleaned up, at least washed his hands and arms. But with his sisters raised, he had a hard time caring about impressing the snotty daughter of the owner of one of the biggest trucking and repair companies in the country.

Riley could come to him. He didn't give a flip, because he was quitting.

Chapter Two

Riley's heels clicked on the pavement. She carried her purse, not because she needed it, but because it helped to keep her hands still if she were holding something. Over the years, she'd adopted many tricks for looking like a polished professional. Her natural personality was anything but. She'd just learned how to do what needed to be done.

The shop wasn't far from the smaller building that housed the offices for the Maine branch of Coleman Trucking, and it took less than a minute to walk there. Still, she was grateful for her jacket. At least Pennsylvania didn't cling to winter like red on blood the way Maine did. It took hardy people to live up here.

An older man carrying a lunch bucket pushed the man door open.

"Oh." Riley stumbled back. "Excuse me."

"No. Excuse me, ma'am." The man tipped his ball cap and walked through, holding the door so Riley could enter.

"Thanks."

It took her eyes a moment to adjust to the dimmer interior. There were three bays. This shop was so good, it was where the company sent their rebuilds if at all possible. It looked like there were two current ones.

Finally she saw movement over by the far truck. A white t-shirt stood out against the gloom. She took a deep breath, pulled from her years of dealing with her dad, and started over. Her future hinged on the outcome of this meeting. She wasn't exactly Ben Baxter's favorite person. Although she'd come a long way from that disastrous day years ago, he didn't know. She'd never gone back and tried to make it right. Once it was done, there was no point in dredging up past hurts.

When she'd come back from college and started working at the shop, she'd looked for a way to try. But he never acted like he cared, and she didn't want to rock the boat. He was the best mechanic their company had. He was the reason the shop performed so well. Of course, Riley was good at her job, but she knew most of the credit belonged to Ben. If she had approached him and it hadn't gone well, he might have quit.

They both pretended nothing ever happened. The little bit that they saw each other, they treated the other with professional respect.

She didn't want him to quit. She didn't want their company to lose their most valuable employee. Sure. But there was another reason, a bigger reason, she never said anything.

It would have been too dangerous to her traitorous heart.

After all the time that had gone by without explanation or apology, she couldn't expect him to believe the best of her now.

The click of her heels echoed in the cavernous interior. Firm and purposeful. Just like she wanted.

The white shirt moved. Ben's face came into focus. As always, something hot and sweet burst in her chest when she looked at him. Ruthlessly she shoved it down. She'd ruined any chance of a relationship. Brutally and on purpose. Now she had to live with her choice.

"Hello, Ben."

Without responding, he wiped his hands, shoved the rag in his pocket, and crossed his arms.

She squeezed her purse and tried for a friendly smile. She really needed this man.

"Thanks so much for meeting me." She wouldn't mention that she'd asked for him to come to her, and while he hadn't refused, he'd said that he'd be working late to pull a motor out. Did she want the truck fixed or did she want him in her office?

His chin might have lifted a fraction.

So, no pleasantries. Of course not. She'd get right down to business.

"What you've done in this shop over the last four years has been beyond amazing." He was an amazing foreman. But he wouldn't have been successful if she hadn't given him the reins to do what he needed to do. One of which was doing actual work himself. That was a huge red flag to HR, but Riley had made it work because Ben had been right—the guys under him worked better if he was working too. He filled the position of shop foreman and head mechanic. He'd trained several men over the last few years to his level. Then the bigger shops had stolen them.

He didn't respond. Not even an eyebrow movement. He wouldn't have any trouble talking to her dad.

She jumped back in. "The biggest shop we have—the one in Pennsylvania, just outside of Brickley Springs—is also our worst-performing one. I know you can turn it around. I'm here to offer you the position of shop foreman."

"Wouldn't work."

She ignored him. "I'm going, too. Together we can implement the arrangement we have here. It's a bigger shop. We'll have some more red tape to cut through..."

"No."

"I know we..."

"Hate each other's guts?" he offered helpfully.

The first ever hint that they had history. She wouldn't allow the clenching of her heart to distract her from her purpose.

She lifted her chin. "Had a misunderstanding and don't get on well."

"You call that a misunderstanding?" He snorted and leaned back against the corner of his massive toolbox.

She pulled her lips out from between her teeth, ignoring him. It wasn't a misunderstanding at all. She'd been brutal. Because she had to. "We make a great team. You know this terminal is the best in the company. I want us to go to Pennsylvania and make that one even better."

"I disagree," he said, with a slight mocking tone in his voice.

She ignored the tone along with the implication that they didn't make a great team. "That's fine. We don't have to agree on everything."

A few beats of silence thumped between them.

"It will be a major salary increase, of course." Money would do it every time. Ben wasn't any different than any other single dad, although technically he wasn't a dad. She'd met his sisters, of course. Spruce Mountain, Maine, wasn't the smallest town in the world, but because of the freedom she'd given Ben to work and manage as he saw fit, his twin sisters were around the shop. Less now that they were older. Nice girls.

"Not interested." His arms came down, and he straightened like the conversation was over.

Riley's heart quaked. She needed Ben.

"It will be triple your current salary."

Ben smiled, his white teeth flashing, contrasting against his tanned skin. "Not interested."

She had to hide the quaking in her heart. There was no way she could do what needed to be done without Ben. Obviously she was going to have to find another way to talk him into it. She couldn't admit defeat. "I'll give you a few days to think about it."

Before he could turn that down, too, she spun and hurried away.

"Hey, watch…"

Ben's warning faded out as Riley cut around the truck too close and hit the corner of the fender. It didn't hurt at first, but that stretching feeling when skin separates made bile back up in her throat. Warmth seeped down her lower leg.

Rustling behind her, a muted ripping sound like paper towels being torn, then Ben was beside her, kneeling.

Blood ran down her leg, and he dabbed it with the clean towel in his hand. All the feelings that she'd fought and ignored for the past years ripped open, and she jerked back.

"It's fine." Her voice quivered, and she didn't even care. She just had to get away from him. She backed up and turned as he stood slowly, the towel held in a hand fisted with white knuckles. Catching just a glimpse of resignation on his face, she headed toward the door, her heels clipping double time.

She didn't stop until she was out in the fading sunlight, the door slamming behind her. The cold air hit her leg, and she felt every centimeter where the blood had seeped down. It wasn't so bad that it would need stitches. She'd seen enough injuries to know it hadn't cut deep enough. The thing that really needed to be stitched back together was her pride. Seeing him was bad enough. She couldn't stand for him to touch her. She'd end up on her knees begging him to take her back.

She straightened. No, she wouldn't. High school was a long time ago. They'd both changed into different people. They didn't know each other anymore. She was still moved by the memories, not by the actual man.

Two heads bobbed across the parking lot toward her, and she shoved the pinching pain in her leg aside.

Eve and Eden. Ben's sisters. Riley knew them well and also knew that Ben would do anything for them. Something had happened to their parents—Riley was sketchy on the details—and Ben had raised them.

"Hey, girls." Riley stopped and offered a friendly smile. Ben might have a grizzly bear personality, but his sisters were sweet.

"Miss Riley," Eden, the blond twin, said. "Did you get transferred to the shop?"

Riley gave a carefree laugh, shoving the last of her lingering troubles aside. "I think we all know I'd be helpless in there."

"And your family owns a trucking company." Eden shook her head then laughed, too. "I'd be helpless in there as well, even though Ben runs the place."

Eve was the twin who took after her brother. Eve fixed trucks. Eden painted them.

"Did Ben get in trouble?" Eve asked with a frown.

"No." Riley tucked a stray hair behind her ear. It was getting chilly out now that the sun had sunk behind the mountain. "I had a proposition for him."

"Yes! I knew it! I always knew you two were meant for each other!" Eve did a little hop then high-fived her twin.

"Not that kind of proposition." Riley laughed at the twins' exuberance. "You're trying to push your brother off?"

"All he's ever done is take care of us. He needs a life."

"Maybe he's happy here." Yeah, the guy was gorgeous, and she felt a definite attraction, but she wouldn't wish his grumpy, miserable personality on any woman. At least that's what she told herself.

Wait. What was she saying? She cleared her throat. "Or maybe he'd like a change of scenery. There's a job opening in Pennsylvania, and I offered it to him."

"Did he jump on it?" Eden asked eagerly.

"He turned it down."

"Why?" Eden asked, shoving her hands in her back pockets.

Riley lifted a shoulder and adjusted her purse, thinking about Ben's flat refusal. "He didn't say."

The twins shared a look which made hope blossom in Riley's heart. Then it sank.

Eve's lip pulled back. "I think you're right. Ben's happy here in Maine."

Eden nodded in agreement, with a similar look. "Yeah. He isn't the kind of guy who likes to pull up roots and travel around."

Riley didn't want to cause strife in their family. They'd already had it hard enough. But she really needed Ben. "That's too bad. It was a great opportunity."

"More money?" Eve asked with a lifted brow.

Riley nodded. Complete honesty. "A lot more money."

Their heads bobbed slowly, but neither seemed interested, and Riley was ready to give up hope that they would help her convince their brother to take the job.

She gave it another plug. "It's our company's biggest terminal, and Ben would have the highest shop position in the company."

Eve's expression grew crafty. "So if that's such a prestigious place to be, will you ever get promoted to there?"

Riley grinned. "I actually got promoted too."

Eden's mouth opened in an "o." "You're moving to Pennsylvania?"

"I'm supposed to within the month."

The twins looked at each other again. An expression Riley couldn't read. Despite the cooling air, she didn't move to walk away. There was something in that look she didn't understand, but it encouraged her for some reason.

"Did Ben know that you were going too?" Eden asked casually.

Riley snorted and looked off at distant mountains. "I think that was one reason he didn't want to. He'd finally be rid of me."

"No. He doesn't feel that way."

Riley's head snapped back around, and she studied the twins.

"Yeah, he's said a lot of times how he wouldn't be successful in his job if you hadn't bent or changed the rules to accommodate his changes."

Thoughts flew through her head. She'd always had a good relationship with the twins. They'd eaten in her office a few times, and she'd even taken them out for lunch when they'd been around and Ben couldn't stop working. But she always assumed that Ben had presented her in the worst possible light and they were just being nice.

It was possible, she supposed, that Ben had never told the twins what she'd done to him. After all these years, it was too late for her to change it or take it back, even if he had told. What's done was done. "Well, I appreciate that. But I still think that he'll be happy to see the last of me."

Chapter Three

Ben set a bowl of spaghetti on the table. The little house he'd moved into at fourteen when he'd run away from his dad's home after finding out his real mother lived in Maine was small but cozy. He'd not changed anything after his mother had died from complications from lupus, and his sisters weren't interested in redecorating, either. Which meant the kitchen was comfortably outdated and gently worn. Not that he usually paid too much attention to the décor. He made sure everything worked—faucets fixed, cabinet doors screwed tight, and the drawers slid easily on their runners. But if the wallpaper was a faded yellow or if the fixtures were corroded, hey, at least the water came out and the lights came on. That's all he cared about.

Except Riley was leaving Maine.

And she wanted him to go too.

Aside from Riley, he had a strong pull in Pennsylvania. His gram had been in poor health for years. She wanted him to come home. She wanted to meet the twins who didn't even know she existed. Major coincidence that the Coleman Trucking and Repair home terminal was in Brickley Springs, his father's hometown and where his gram still lived.

Actually, not so coincidental. Brickley Springs was ideally suited for commerce. Directly between the PA Turnpike and I80, one could go anywhere—east, west, north, or south—and fast, from Brickley Springs. It was a smart place to put a terminal. It was a great place for a truck driver, like his dad, to live.

He glanced around the kitchen again as Eve put parmesan cheese on the table and Eden pulled the garlic bread out of the oven.

He supposed this wasn't much of a home. Not to someone who grew up in a mansion with millions. Riley had made it perfectly clear years ago that he wasn't good enough. That had been enough to keep him from pursuing her but not enough to keep him from noticing her.

His fingers tingled, and he gripped the plastic cups tighter. He'd touched her today. Hadn't mean to. Hadn't touched her in years. Shouldn't have done it.

"You're quiet tonight." Eve poured sweet tea into the cups he'd set down.

"Oh, forgot." He snapped up like he'd just remembered something important. "I'm supposed to drill you about your day."

"No," they said together.

He ignored the protest. He'd gotten good at ignoring protests over the years. "Did you show up on time and put in a full day's work?"

"Ben." Eve rolled her eyes.

"What? Was today the class day?" He couldn't remember. One day a week, Eden had class instruction, and the rest of the time, she was in the shop doing hands-on work, learning to run the different airbrushes and how to get the base coats on. Auto detail painting wasn't hard, but it was exact. Which was good for Eden. Who knew where her loads of artistic talent came from, but she needed the discipline of forcing herself to do the grunt work, too.

"Ben, I'm out of high school and almost done with trade school. Your job is over."

"You're never done being a parent." He said it in a scholarly voice like he was reading it out of a parenting book.

Eden lifted her brows before chucking him on the shoulder. "Brother. You're never done being a brother."

"Well, I had a good day," Eve said, running interference with her twin, like he didn't notice. "And you can grill me on it if you want."

Ben paused with his fork midair. "Did that what's-his-face keep his fingers to himself?"

"After I set his pants on fire with the hand torch."

Ben matched her grin. "Glad you listen to me, girl."

She pushed her spaghetti around on her plate. "Mitch said I could start on motors next month if I keep on doing as well as I've been doing on brakes and oil changes."

"You didn't tell him you already know how to gut it and rebuild?"

"No. I'm hoping he'll help me with the electrical parts. These new motors are all computerized, and you only worked with me on the old stuff."

"That's what the independent guys want. If you don't work for a big shop, you'll be seeing a lot of old stuff."

"Why did you turn Riley down?" Eden asked.

After raising his sisters for the last decade and a half, he should be used to these sudden topic changes. His head still spun. Probably more from thinking about Riley than the abrupt change in subject.

"She told us it was a huge promotion for you."

"Yeah. Apparently the shop in Pennsylvania is much bigger than the one you're at now."

He hated it when they ganged up on him like this. As always, he tried not to let them know it bothered him. "You guys know I've always said after you're out of school I was going to open my own place. I'm planning on quitting." Plus, they didn't exactly know that they had family in Pennsylvania. If he moved to Brickley Springs, he'd have to tell them. They'd have to meet Gram.

It wasn't like the town was so big they'd never hear about someone else with the same last name. His brother's first names didn't exactly fade into the woodwork, either.

He hid his smirk, waiting until Eve was seated before he said, "Let's pray."

It always bothered him when someone decided to use the dinner table blessing to pray for their Great-aunt Mildred and the health and well-being of all their seventeen cousins. Not that there wasn't a time and place to have a long chat with the Lord. Just not while his food was getting cold.

It was only a few seconds later that he said "amen," and Eve started like they'd never been interrupted.

"I'd like to go south."

He should have prayed for Great-aunt Mildred.

"It would be warmer there," Eden chimed in.

Ben dished himself some spaghetti. "No seafood in PA."

They weren't deterred. "But warmth more months of the year than August," Eden argued, giving him the cheese and taking some garlic bread for herself.

"True," he said, shoving food in his mouth, hoping to set an example that his sisters would follow. They were sliding into dangerous territory as long as they were talking about Pennsylvania.

"How do you know?" Both twins' eyes moved to him and stayed. He hated it when they looked at him like that.

He swallowed, having avoided this confession their whole lives. "I lived there before I knew about my mom and you guys." A little pang hit his chest. They had uncles—his half brothers. But if those guys had turned out anything like their dad, he wanted his sisters far away from them. Which is exactly the reason he'd never told them about the family. Gram had mentioned once that the oldest, Torque, was in prison. After that, he'd said he didn't want to talk about them. No way was he letting his sisters around men like that, even if they were their half brothers.

When Gram had first reached out to him, he'd told her the twins didn't know about their Pennsylvania relatives, and it needed to stay that way if she wanted him to pick up the phone when she called. At first, he'd not cared much about Gram—she was part of his old life with his dad, which he'd left. But the woman was stubborn and gritty and truly cared about him and his sisters. She'd wormed her way into his heart, and he loved her fiercely.

He'd been tempted over the years to at least tell them about Gram, but being a brother and single parent to twins was hard enough. He didn't need to add any more drama to his life. He didn't want to go to Pennsylvania. Because Riley was in Maine.

"You lived there?" Eden asked incredulously.

He ignored Eden's question, but Eve was like a dog with a bone, and she fired off, "Why not move to Pennsylvania, work at the big shop, and see if you like it? You could always start your own shop in another year or so if you decide you wanted to."

"It's not like you hate your job or anything," Eden tag-teamed her.

He shoved more spaghetti in his mouth and ignored them.

They were right. He didn't hate his job. But he did chafe at the restrictions. Something in him wanted to be his own boss. To prove he could do it. No better time than now, when his sisters were no longer dependent on him for everything.

"Maybe you'd find a girl down there," Eve said with a sly grin.

"Yeah." Eden jabbed her fork in the air to press her point. "Now that you can't use us as an excuse anymore."

He swallowed, tilting his head. "I never used you as an excuse."

"You sure did. We'd ask why you didn't marry, and you'd say you couldn't find a girl who wanted a ready-made family."

"I was kidding." Although it had been true. Most girls pretended to like his sisters but weren't really interested in raising kids that weren't their own. Heck, a lot of women didn't even want their own kids. Plus, there was only one woman who had ever challenged him to the depths of his soul. Too bad she'd scorched her way there.

Their looks said they didn't believe him.

He held up the hand that held his garlic bread. "Okay, fine. I used you as an excuse."

They looked smug.

Eve said, "And now you don't have us as an excuse anymore."

"So you can take the job in Pennsylvania."

He lifted a brow at Eden. "You're gonna hurt someone with that fork."

Surprise flashed across Eden's face, chased by a sheepish grin. She jabbed her utensil into her spaghetti.

He relented. "Okay. Say I did take it." He eyed them over his spaghetti. "And I move to PA. Where are you two going to live?"

They looked at each other, and he felt a surge of triumph. Ha. They hadn't thought of that.

Then Eve shrugged. "We'll come with you."

Chapter Four

Ben walked into the Coleman shop at five a.m., flipping on the lights and turning up the heat. He started coffee in the cold pot. There was no night shift at this shop.

There would be in Pennsylvania.

He pushed that thought out of his head. Maybe a little of him was tempted to go, but if he were being honest with himself, the main temptation for him was because Riley was going. He didn't even really like her, even if he was attracted to her, but he'd kind of gotten used to having her around. That's what he told himself anyway.

He wasn't going to follow her around like a lovesick puppy. She'd kicked him out of the way with her high-dollar shoes once. No one had ever accused him of being a slow learner.

He stood on the frame rails of the gutted truck from last night and had just slipped the liner in piston number ten when the door opened with a blast of cold air. Odd, since his guys weren't scheduled to come in until seven, and none of them ever showed up at six, which was about what time it should be. He couldn't know for sure since he wasn't wearing a watch and his phone lay over on the worktable with the pieces of the big diesel engine that he'd torn down yesterday.

The light click of heels echoed off the high ceiling of the garage, and

Ben's body had the same odd reaction it always did when Riley came near. His heart thundered, while dread pooled in his stomach. His brain began issuing rapid-fire instructions to stay away, keep the walls up, don't let her in, while his mouth went dry and his whole body ached to draw closer.

He tapped the liner. This job needed precision and concentration. Maybe she'd leave.

"Ben."

"Riley," he said without looking up. He needed to go get another liner, but he'd rather stand above her than get down and go fetch it, so he pretended to be busy.

"You can quit pretending you're busy. I might not know much, but I know the tapper you're holding isn't used anywhere near that bolt you're playing with."

Busted. He straightened. "You need something? 'Cause some of us around here actually work. While some of us just sit in our office keeping Daddy happy." That was low, and he felt bad as soon as the words were out of his mouth. Normally people considered him nice. Riley brought out the bitterness he still harbored.

If his barbs hit their mark, her face didn't flinch. Carefully bland. "I just figured I'd ask if you changed your mind."

He put his hand on the windshield and looked down at her. "You know, I actually did think about that last night. You can't do what needs to be done without me."

To her credit, she looked him in the eye. Thankfully she couldn't see his brain going around like the fins of a turbo.

"I can't." Her chin jutted out. "You're right. The shop needs to be turned around. I know I can handle the office side of things, and I can get things set up so you can work your magic outside."

He narrowed his eyes. She was patronizing him.

She threw a hand up. "I'm serious. I know you don't like me..." This time, she did look away. She caught her lips between her teeth. He'd almost kissed those lips. A long time ago.

Squaring her shoulders, she turned back to face him. "I'm sorry." Her face seemed sincere. Something else flitted across it. Something that looked like regret. He had to have read it wrong. "I know what I did was...rude."

He waved his hand, dismissing her words. He wasn't going to admit, not for anything, that the way she'd dumped him still hurt. He wasn't carrying a torch for her, and he didn't really even like her. Other than the dumb attraction he felt every time she was in the room. "Forget it. It's history. If you're still thinking about it, you need to let it go."

If his heart had eyes, they'd be rolling right now. But he kept his face clear.

"I wanted you to know—"

"Forget it." Maybe his words came out a little more forcefully than they needed to.

Her mouth hung open before she snapped it shut. Her face lost the vulnerable look, and his stomach tightened because he was the one who'd erased that soft sweetness that sat so beautifully on her.

Her eyes narrowed. "Fine. When you're ready to let me explain, I'm ready to tell you."

He shook his head.

Then, because he needed another liner, he stepped on the steer tire and jumped down. She stepped back.

"Is that all you wanted?" he asked dismissively. He'd never get anything accomplished if he had to fight the desire to look at her constantly.

She waited so long to answer he thought she wasn't going to. "You're right. I need you. Will you reconsider?"

"Nope."

She pressed her lips together and turned.

He didn't watch her walk away.

Chapter Five

R iley stepped into her office and shut the door, leaning against it. She had her own office here, at least. It wasn't a corner office, and this was their smallest terminal. But it was better than being in an open room with flimsy partitions separating her from her coworkers. Which is where she could end up if she didn't manage to do the impossible thing her dad was demanding of her.

She blew out a breath. That visit was a fail. Without Ben, she couldn't do what her dad wanted her to. There was no way. Even if Ben would help her make the changes necessary without actually taking the job, she might have a chance.

But he didn't want to have anything to do with her. Maybe if she could have explained why she'd done what she did, but she'd let it go for so long. He probably wouldn't believe her anyway. And a few sentences of explanation wouldn't erase years of resentment. She'd never done anything more, but she hadn't needed to.

A tap on her door startled her. She straightened her shoulders. She'd just have to do it by herself. Or find someone else like Ben. Like there was anyone else in the world like Ben.

Brushing her hands down her skirt, she turned and opened the door. "Hey, Audrey. Come on in."

Her personal secretary stepped through the doorway gingerly. "He said no?"

Riley nodded.

Audrey's face fell. Even though no one else was in that early, she finished walking in and closed the door behind her. She tilted her head. "Maybe you're not giving yourself enough credit? Maybe you can do this without Ben."

Riley forced her lips to turn up. "Thanks for the support. I've learned a lot over the past few years, but Ben is the reason the shop is successful."

"Maybe his way of doing things wouldn't work in Pennsylvania. I mean, they're a different breed down there." She shrugged. "It takes a certain kind of hardiness to live in Maine."

They smiled. Survivors of Maine's unforgiving and unending winters.

"It's not for everyone," Riley agreed. She pushed her hair back. "I appreciate you trying, but we both know without Ben I'm never going to be able to do what my dad expects."

Audrey fingered the folders in her hand. "Then maybe it's time you stopped trying."

Riley stared at her. Stop trying to please her dad? But she worked for his company. She planned to run it someday. "I can't. I might as well quit today and find a new job. He's not just my dad, he's my boss."

"It doesn't matter what he is. You can't do impossible things for him." Audrey wrapped her arms around the folders and held them close to her chest. "I'm not trying to tell you to rebel against your dad. Of course, you can't do that. But every time he tells you to do something, no matter how impossible, you kill yourself trying to impress him." Audrey's eyes softened. Her voice lowered. "He never appreciates it, just acts like that's what he expected."

Riley's mind reeled. In today's world, it was perfectly acceptable to thumb one's nose at one's parents. That didn't make it right. She couldn't do it, although it was difficult to put words as to why. "That's what makes me feel so good—like Dad knows I can do it and doesn't expect anything less from me. I wouldn't be as good as I am if it weren't for his high expectations."

"I just thought you might be tired of trying to meet those high expectations. Especially when he doesn't appreciate you. Also, when you need other people to uproot their lives so you don't disappoint your dad...."

Riley sighed and walked to her window, looking out on the closed garage bay. "You're definitely right about that. I can't expect other people to help me meet Dad's unreasonable expectations." She turned. "I didn't ask you to come." She gave Audrey a meaningful look. "And I offered Ben a huge promotion. It's not like he was giving up a good job and salary to work for peanuts while I built an empire for my dad."

Audrey looked down at the ground. "You're right. I..." She paused. "I just know you made at least one life-changing mistake because of what your dad thought, and building his business, was more important than...making a life for yourself." Audrey looked Riley square in the eye. "You don't have a life. One day you might regret that."

Audrey was almost certainly talking about what happened with Ben years ago. It was over and done with. Why did it seem like it was haunting her?

Although she was right on more counts, too. Her friend circle had grown smaller and smaller, until she was closer to the people she saw at work than she was with any actual friends. She just didn't have time. There were always reports to compile, data to analyze, employee issues to supervise.

Sure, she had people in place to do all those things, but as the person in charge, she needed to keep her finger in everything. Which she did. Only Ben had free rein to do whatever he wanted. She'd never told him that, but he'd probably figured it out by now. Whatever he decided, she supported. Still, she knew exactly what was going on in the shop. Because she answered to her dad for everything.

She didn't socialize with coworkers, because she was the boss.

Audrey was the closest thing she had to a friend anymore.

She let out a breath and brushed off the front of her skirt. "If that bothers you so much, you should be happy that I asked Ben to move to Pennsylvania with me."

No surprise flickered across Audrey's face. So, office gossip had made the rounds.

Audrey's finger flicked the edge of the folders she held. "Rumor has it that Ben wants to start his own company. Maybe you'd be better off letting someone else take your place and helping him start a business. You said yourself you two make a great team."

A little shot of excitement pinched in her chest. Ben and she could build a successful business. She was sure of it. She pursed her lips. "Problem is, Ben didn't ask me." She allowed a small, meaningful pause. "I did ask him. He said no."

"Maybe Ben needs the past resolved," Audrey said softly.

"I tried. He wouldn't listen."

"Maybe you should make him."

She loved Audrey, and she'd miss her. Miss having someone so close to her who wasn't afraid to speak her mind and didn't hold it against Riley that sometimes she was an idiot. But it did get tiring having one's conscience in one's face all the time.

"I think it's just best if we let that go. I'm leaving. He's not. And right now, my biggest problem is that I need someone as good as Ben to be my shop manager."

Audrey held out the folders. "I went through several employment portals last night. Nationwide. I printed off pertinent info. One folder for each prospect."

Riley took the folders. The ball in her chest eased slightly. "Thanks so much."

Audrey didn't let go of the folders right away. She waited for Riley to look at her. "But you're not going to find someone like Ben. And I'm not just talking about an employee."

Riley's heart had to agree with that. She squeezed the folders tighter than necessary. "He hates me."

"There's a fine line between love and hate."

~

"Heard the boss lady was packing up and heading to the BS terminal." Danny slapped the hood of the truck Ben stood beside, up to his elbows in rods and pistons.

"Hmm." Ben kept his head down, focused on working in the tight space without pinching his fingers any more than necessary.

"Hope they don't hire a jerk to take her place."

Ben grunted. His wrench slipped off, the grease making it difficult to get a solid hold. He tried again.

"She pretty much lets us do whatever we want. Heck, if we worked at any other shop, you'd be sitting on your little throne, watching us minions work."

Ben stopped and looked at Danny. "Versus this one where you sit on the throne and watch me work?" He pulled a lip back, not sure how effective his expression was with all the grease that had to be on his face.

Danny laughed but walked on. "I can take a hint, Bossman. I've already changed a rear and a turbo today."

"You get that tranny pulled out before twelve, and lunch is on me." Ben smiled to himself. Danny could do it, but he'd not be able to stop and talk the rest of the morning.

"It'll be done," he called from the other side of the shop. "You better get your big pocketbook out."

Ben laughed, knowing Danny would probably just want hot dogs from the corner gas station. He'd want to go get them, too, because he thought the cashier was cute.

The other two guys in the shop joined in, teasing that Ben used hundred-dollar bills as toilet paper. After a couple more shouted challenges and insults, things settled down and the guys were putting a push on to see who'd get the most done before lunch.

Ben set a bolt on the steer tire and reached in to get the other one off. Things were running really well here. He'd done the best job he could do. He'd figured, now that the twins were grown, it was time to move on, but he'd been dragging his feet. Change was hard, but he wasn't afraid of it.

He knew why he hadn't moved. She was a hundred yards away in the office across the parking lot. Stupid heart of his fell one time and wouldn't give up. He hadn't been able to get it to beat for anyone else, hard as he tried.

Maybe if he stayed here and Riley moved to Pennsylvania, he'd finally be able to get her out of his mind.

Or maybe if he moved to Pennsylvania, they'd finally be able to get past the issue that had lain between them like Antarctica—uncrossable, except for the strongest and most determined person. It's what he wanted, but he didn't think he could swallow his pride enough to follow the woman who'd humiliated him across six states like a lovesick dog.

Chapter Six

L ater that week, Ben sat out on the cold porch swing by himself. He leaned against the armrest, one boot propped on the swing, one solid on the floor, pushing slowly. It was still cold but not the frigid cold of a Maine winter. Forty degrees was relative.

The twins had gone out with their friends. He never went to bed until they were home. Yeah, they might be over eighteen and all that, but there was no way he'd be able to sleep until he knew they were safe.

His phone buzzed at his side, and he jumped like he always did, his first thought it was the police. Or the morgue.

One glance at the number had his forehead wrinkling. He didn't recognize the area code, although it looked familiar.

Two more seconds, then his stomach cramped. He remembered now. It was a Pennsylvania area code, just like Gram's. Not her number.

He swiped the button before reaching behind him and hooking his hand on the swing chain. With his other hand, he put the phone to his ear. "Hello?"

"Is this Ben Baxter?" The female voice was cultured. Like a rich blue blood.

Not sure why such a woman would be calling him, he answered shortly, "Yeah."

"This is Cassidy Baxter."

Baxter. His last name. The woman paused. Ben's mind raced. His dad had no brothers. But...this could be his...sister-in-law?

He waited.

"I'm married to Torque."

Torque was the oldest of his three half brothers. His dad had given the three younger boys weird truck names. Occasionally Ben had wondered how he'd escaped that curse, but what he'd found that caused him to run had given him all the answers he needed.

He'd always assumed his brothers would turn out just like their dad, and Ben couldn't save everyone, so he'd focused on his sisters. His full-blooded sisters. But this woman, Cassidy, had an educated edge to her voice.

"I'm your sister-in-law."

He rolled his eyes. Maybe she did think he was stupid since he wasn't saying anything. "I figured. Torque, Tough, and Turbo." His half brothers. They were always in the back of his mind. Especially since he'd been talking to his gram. She'd never mentioned them other than the one time she'd said Torque was in prison and he'd threatened to hang up if she ever mentioned them again. She'd never made him feel bad for not visiting or having any contact. That hadn't stopped him from telling the biggest lie of his life to her several years ago.

"That's right. Tough and Turbo are both married too." She cleared her throat. "Anyway, I'm sure you realize I used the internet to find you. I've had your contact information for a while." Her voice softened. "I know Torque would love to talk to you, but that's not why I'm calling."

"Okay." His little brother would love to talk to him. His little brother, who had been in *prison*, who was married to this articulate, cultured woman. It made him curious.

"I'm at the hospital. They think Gram had a heart attack last night."

Ben's heart rammed to a stop. Guilt that he had never taken his sisters to meet her, never even told them about her, tightened his throat. His boot thudded off the swing onto the porch. The chain cut into his fingers.

Cassidy continued, "She asked for you." She paused. "She wants to see you. And your wife and sisters."

Gram. He'd neglected her in favor of his mother and sisters. And now she lay dying in a hospital. He couldn't swallow the lump in his throat. Guilt.

She wanted to see his sisters. He could do that. His wife? Um...

Lying was never the solution. He could remember his mother saying that on her deathbed as clearly as though she sat on the swing in the dark with him this second. It had been when he'd said he was going to get a job, and he was going to lie on the application and say he was eighteen instead of sixteen. He hadn't felt he had any other choice, since his dad was gone and his mother was dying. If he hadn't lied, he wouldn't have been able to keep his sisters.

The lie to his gram...not as necessary. She'd asked if he'd ever gotten married, and he'd said, "yes." Stupid, stupid man.

Such a dumb, unnecessary lie. He just didn't want her to think he was like his dad, moving from woman to woman to woman. A wife and children in one state. A wife and children in another state. *At the same time.*

There were laws against that. God's laws. Man's laws. He wanted to be different. Lying had been a stupid solution.

Cassidy was silent on the other end.

Tell her the truth.

But he didn't want to admit to lying. And he didn't want to admit to losing a wife he never had. He'd been worried about his brothers turning out like their dad. Maybe they were worried about the same thing with him. He was the oldest, too. He couldn't lose face. It would be hard enough to go back and face the family he'd run from. He couldn't do it from a position of weakness.

Finally Cassidy spoke again. "The doctors aren't sure how much longer she'll last. She's stable, and they're conducting tests, but it's touchy."

Ben leaned his head back, looking up at the porch ceiling. He couldn't disappoint his gram. His dad had never given two hoots about him. His mother was gone. Gram was the only adult in his family who had ever cared.

But he couldn't stand to have her find out he'd lied. That he didn't really have a family, didn't even have a life, to be honest.

Headlights cut through the night. A car turned slowly into their short drive. The twins were home.

Ben felt like the world was closing in on him.

He had to tell Eve and Eden they had a grandmother who was alive and wanted to see them. He had to admit to his gram he wasn't married and never had been. And after he'd so bluntly turned down Riley's offer of a promotion, he needed to ask for extended time off.

Normally he hoarded his vacation like a pack rat, but he'd used it all up for the year this past summer when the twins and he had taken the trip of a lifetime. They'd gone across the country and seen the Grand Canyon, Yellowstone, the Pacific Ocean, and a ton of other sights they'd all only dreamed about. It had been the best time ever. But he had zero vacation time left.

Double crap.

"You know what? I don't know why I even called. This was a total waste of time." Cassidy's cultured voice throbbed with irritation. "I'm sorry I bothered you," she said, not sounding the slightest bit sorry but sounding a lot jacked off.

"Wait," he said.

She quit talking, but the silence, even over the phone, pulsed with judgment and anger.

"I'm just...surprised. I'll be down to see Gram."

"With your family." The words could have been cut out of diamond, sharp edges and all hardness.

Ben closed his eyes. "With my family."

Cassidy rattled off the name of the hospital and the room number. "I'll text it to you," she added, like she didn't want to give him any excuses for not showing up.

"Thanks."

"When should I tell her you'll be here?"

Car doors slammed. The twins would be out here in less than a minute. He needed to figure out what he was going to tell them. What *was* he going to tell them?

"Soon."

"Lovely," Cassidy said, the one word dripping with sarcasm. Then her voice changed. "I don't know you or anything about you, but I do know you have three brothers here who would really like to know you and your family." She paused. "I'll see you. Soon."

Then she hung up.

Ben dropped his phone into his lap, stretching both hands behind his head and holding onto the swing chain.

Why had he lied?

What was he going to do about it now?

Chapter Seven

E den walked out on the porch, holding a cup in her hands, followed by Eve.

"Hot tea?" Eden asked.

"No, thanks." He was anything but cold. Ever since his phone rang, his heart had been pumping like pistons in a freight train.

"You know you don't have to wait up for us anymore. We're big girls." Eve sat down on the chair at the opposite end of the swing. Eden stood, sipping her drink.

"Yeah. I know," he said without lifting his head. "Have a good night?"

"It was good. Carrie's fighting with her mother who's fighting with her two sisters." Eve laughed. "I guess it's good we don't have family. Can't fight with 'em if you don't have 'em."

"Well, about that." Ben dropped his hands from the swing chain and shifted. He braced his forearms on his knees. "I have a few things to tell you."

"You decided to take the job in Pennsylvania after all?"

He snorted. That job was the least of his worries. "No." He swallowed. "But I guess I never mentioned that you have family in Pennsylvania."

The girls gasped.

Familiar with their brains after so many years together, he spoke before they could attack him with questions. "We have three half brothers, their wives, and a grandmother."

"No way!"

"You're kidding."

"Why didn't you tell us?"

"'I guess I never mentioned?'" Eve parroted in a voice dripping with sarcasm and anger.

He ignored their outbursts. Sometimes that was the only way he could deal with them. "Your grandmother is in the hospital. They think she had a heart attack, and she's stable. They're doing some testing."

They were quiet for a bit, adjusting. Maybe back when they were teens, they might have stomped off. Maybe even given him the silent treatment for a while. But thankfully, they'd matured.

He hadn't been the best parent in the world, had made tons of mistakes. This was probably one of the biggest.

"When a kid has a grandparent, you don't keep it from them," Eve said in a tone that indicated this was one of the many areas he'd messed up in as a parent.

He pulled on the swing chain, flexing his biceps and working some of the frustration out. Eve and Eden had turned out okay—great, really —in spite of his faults and failures. "I'm sorry," he said softly.

"An apology really isn't sufficient when we're talking about *grandparents*." Eden crossed her arms over her chest.

"I can't change it. I did what I thought needed to be done in order to protect you."

"How is keeping our grandmother away from us 'protecting' us?" Eve used one hand to do air quotes around "protecting."

"Our dad..." He hated to speak ill of the dead.

"Wait." Eve still sat on the chair, her tea held, forgotten, in her hands. "We have brothers? Like, Dad had—"

"He had another wife, another whole family, in Pennsylvania."

"That's illegal!" Eden practically shouted.

"Yeah." It was wrong on so many levels, but it was illegal as well. "Dad was not a good guy. He lied and cheated. He was a drunkard with a nasty temper. He couldn't hold a steady job. I don't want to go on, but yeah, this was one of the things he did that I didn't see the point in telling you about."

"But they're our family!"

"I don't know anything about them." He didn't think he wanted to mention that one of them was in prison. It would help his argument, but it seemed like overkill. "They could be just like Dad, and my job was to raise you. I couldn't deal with whatever drama the rest of the family produced."

The girls were quiet. Ben closed his eyes and leaned his head back against the chain. "I'm sorry. Maybe I should have told you. But I did the best I could."

A few seconds ticked by that felt like an eternity. Finally, Eve said, "It's okay, Ben. If you hadn't been here for us, I don't know what would have happened."

"Yeah." Eden's voice was small. "I'm sorry I was upset. I guess I was thinking how much I wanted to have a grandmother like my friends had, and cousins and family, but I guess I really don't know what they're like."

"And they're so far away, we wouldn't have seen them much anyway," Ben pointed out.

Eve popped up. Liquid splashed on the floor. "We've got to go see her."

"Does she know about us?" Eden asked softly.

Ben swallowed, hating to admit the truth but already having to deal with the aftereffects of one lie. Which was one too many. "I've talked to her off and on, maybe once a month, for the last few years. She really wants to see you, and I've just made excuses."

"I can't believe you didn't tell us this." Eden crossed her arms over her chest. Her voice was shot through with irritation.

"I can't believe we haven't gone to see her." Eve walked over and stood beside her twin. When they did that, it always felt like it was two against one. Always before, he'd stood firm because he knew he was right. This time, he'd been wrong and he knew it.

And now the worst part. His chest tightened, and his neck crawled. "I told her I had a wife and my wife couldn't travel because of her job."

The girls gasped. Eve actually took a step back, her arms falling. "You what?"

"You heard me."

"I did. I just can't believe it. You lied." Eve put both fists on her hips.

"Not only did he lie, he lied to our *grandmother*." Eden's arms dropped to her sides. "We have a grandmother." She turned to her twin and threw her arms around her. They danced around in a circle, tea splashing on the floor.

Ben smiled a little to see their enthusiasm, but his head drooped down.

Eventually they remembered him.

Eve pointed her finger at him. "You are going to have to go right down there and admit to your grandmother that you lied." Her tone perfectly imitated his the time she'd been in seventh grade and he'd found out she cheated on a test. He'd marched her right into her algebra teacher's classroom and forced her to admit that she'd lied and cheated. It had worked, since she'd never done it again.

Unfortunately, he was afraid he was about to get a taste of his own medicine.

"No, he's not." Eden turned and faced him. "Grandmother is in..." She paused. "What do we call her? Grandmother?"

"Gram," he said without looking up.

Eden narrowed her eyes, like she was going to give it to him again, but just nodded and continued. "Gram is in the hospital. *If* we get there before she dies, we don't want her last thought of Ben to be that he lied to her all these years."

Eve tapped a finger on her chin. "I can see your point. He hasn't seen his brothers for years, either. It really wouldn't look good to have him show up and be thought a liar first thing." She glared at Ben. "It's not like he normally lies."

"I can't remember him ever lying to us. Not even about Santa Claus."

Ben gave a little laugh at that. It was true. He'd never lied to the girls. About anything. He was happy about that now. They'd cover for him when he showed up at the hospital without a wife; he could just say she was at home and couldn't get off work. The twins would understand.

He'd have to practice because lying wasn't natural to him, but he could do it.

"So we have to find him a wife."

"And fast."

"Whoa." Ben's head jerked up. "Wait. No. We don't just 'find wives' in a few hours. I've lived thirty-four years and haven't found anyone I want to be shackled to for the rest of my life." Because it really would be for the rest of his life. He'd lived through divorce and adultery and betrayal. It hurt. He wasn't putting his own kids through that. Not for anything.

He wasn't going through it again, either.

"You should have thought of that when you decided it was a good idea to lie in the first place," Eve said in her Imitation Ben Parenting tone.

Ben stood. "Okay, you guys are funny. Ha ha. I'll figure out something. In the meantime..."

"Just wait," Eden said with such authority that he actually stopped and waited. She glanced at her sister who gave a small nod. "If you want our cooperation, you'll need to find a wife."

"Maybe you didn't understand. Gram is in the hospital. She's critical. I don't have time to go wife shopping, even if there were a place where such a thing were for sale."

"Ben." Eden laid a hand on his arm. "You're smart." She paused. "For a man." He rolled his eyes. Why was it always boys against girls? "You can figure this out."

His mind went completely blank. Figure this out? What in the world?

He blinked at them, feeling like he'd stepped into a different degree of reality. Not an uncommon feeling since he'd stepped into the parenting role when their mother died. He ran a hand through his hair. "I guess you give me too much credit. I have no idea what you two are talking about." Women. They did this to him all the time. Most of the time, he knew he was right and ignored them. This time, since he'd been the one to lie to begin with, he wasn't sure where the line was.

Eve laughed. She put her hand on his other arm. "Think about it,

Ben. We know a woman who wants something from you so bad, she'd pretend to be your wife in order to get it."

Ben shook his head. He didn't know any woman who wanted...

Her image popped into his head. Riley. His heart slammed against his ribs like an unsecured load at a stop sign.

He closed his eyes. The knot in his stomach that had burned since he'd gotten Cassidy's call loosened. His lips actually turned up.

"Oh, he's liking the idea."

He couldn't argue with them, but he didn't want them to see him capitulate too easily. They might suspect the truth that lay buried in his soul.

He threw out the first thing that came to mind. "That means I would have to move to Pennsylvania." He'd have to take the job. There really wasn't any part of him that was disappointed about that. It didn't matter how badly she'd humiliated him. Didn't matter that she'd paraded her "daddy-approved" boyfriend down the walk in front of him. Didn't matter that she'd said he'd never be good enough. There would only ever be one woman his soul burned for.

"We'll move with you."

He narrowed his eyes at them, not totally ignorant of their tricks. "You two have been talking about this."

Eve grinned. "We have. We actually didn't have any friends with us tonight."

"It was just us two having a powwow about how to get you to accept Riley's offer."

"You want to move to Pennsylvania?" he asked. The thought had never entered his mind.

They eyed each other and looked down. "Not exactly."

"Spit it," he said, wrapping an arm around each of their shoulders. It hadn't been easy raising them, but it was easy loving them.

"We wanted you to give Riley a chance."

His smile slipped. They didn't know the history between him and Riley. It wasn't really about him giving her a chance. She'd been clear what she wanted, and she'd never indicated her feelings had changed. How could they? She'd been his boss.

Wicked thoughts flew through his mind. A chance. Right. He hid his evil grin.

This would be a way to get back at her. Not that he'd ever been into revenge, but hey… She had thought she was so much better than he was. It would serve her right to have to marry him in order to turn her daddy's shop around and get her corner office promotion.

Could he do that? Could he really stand in front of her and insist that she'd have to marry him to get his help?

Riley could turn him down flat. Marriage was a huge step. She might agree to pretend to be married…but that wouldn't satisfy him. No. It would be too easy for her to walk away. If they didn't have the history between them, he might be okay with a flat exchange—a pretend marriage that was mutually beneficial. But he had an ax to grind, and if he were going to help her, she needed to double pay to cover for what she'd done.

Yeah. A real marriage—one that could be annulled when he moved away from Pennsylvania to start his own business—or no deal. That way she'd be tied to him, humbled. She'd said he wasn't good enough, and her dad had been standing right beside her. It would be sweet revenge to see her dad's face when he found out that his precious daughter had lowered herself to marry him.

He didn't exactly like the idea that marrying him was a punishment, but he did enjoy the irony of the whole situation.

And he had the twins' support. It was hard to resist his evil nature.

The biggest drawback was that the reason he'd lied in the first place was because he didn't want to be like his dad, going from woman to woman to woman. He wanted to be seen as steady and dependable. Moral. This would shoot that in the foot.

But he didn't know what his family was like. If they were decent people, he'd just have to find the courage to tell them he'd lied. And if they weren't, he wouldn't even need to tell them. He'd just disappear again. They would never need to know that the whole thing had been a sham.

He narrowed his eyes at the twins. He'd never lied to them. They'd never seen him be dishonest. He didn't like the idea that they would see it now, but he knew they knew his character. Plus, for some reason, they were stuck on Riley. So, in a way, he could even give them what they wanted. The only thing he'd probably end up lying about would be how long Riley and he'd been married.

"I'll think about it," he finally said to them. "In the meantime, plan on going to class in the morning and making whatever arrangements you can to be away for a few days. You need to go see your gram. I want to be on the way to Pennsylvania sometime after noon tomorrow." Married to Riley or not.

Chapter Eight

R iley dropped into her chair behind her small desk at 7:30 the next morning. She put her head down on the smooth surface. Normally she came into the office rejuvenated and ready to face the new day. Ready for the problems, because there were always problems. She loved the challenge of figuring out solutions, saving money, making people happy—because happy people worked better than unhappy people. Plus, it was just nice to be around happy people.

But this problem...

She reached down, without lifting her head, to dig her laptop out of her bag. In between packing up her apartment, trying to find a replacement for herself here in Maine, getting a jump on the issues in Pennsylvania, and spending more than a little time trying to figure out how to get Ben to change his mind, she'd gone over the files Audrey had given her, setting up interviews for next Monday. She couldn't trust this all-important hire to the normal channels.

There were more than fifty files, and they all looked like good prospects. But a person could look great on paper. It wasn't that hard to fill up a good resume.

Ben, he wouldn't look half as good as some of these guys on an application, but the things that made Ben good at what he did were things that an application couldn't show.

How could she know if any of the applicants could relate to a working man's problems? That they'd know how far and hard to push and when to back off and give a helping hand? That they'd go the extra mile, showing up early, staying late, inspiring devotion and loyalty as Ben did?

It wasn't even something that would show up in an interview. She'd just have to wait and see after they were hired. But she didn't have time to go through a bunch of employees that weren't exemplary. She needed someone like Ben, and she needed them today.

She groaned. Maybe Audrey was right and she tried too hard to please her dad. She'd stop. Right after she got this promotion. *If* she got this promotion.

A rap on her door startled her, and she jerked up, her hand automatically going to smooth her hair down.

She cleared her throat and schooled her features. She had no idea who'd be coming to her office this early in the morning. It definitely wasn't Audrey, who knocked with a gentle tap-tap.

She opened her laptop, thinking to give the impression that she'd been working. "Come in," she called.

Her heart jumped into her throat when Ben walked in the door, his ball cap in his hand. He'd never come to her office without being summoned. Ever.

She tamped down a rise of excitement. Maybe he'd decided to take her offer. It had to be the money. Triple his current salary was a lot of money to a man like Ben.

It hadn't been very often that she'd seen him without his hat on in the past few years. Some guys' hats hid a bald head. Ben's hair was full and just long enough to show a tendency to wave. His features were dark, those brown eyes unreadable. The short stubble gave him a slightly dangerous look, which should not do anything for her but caused her heart to knock against her ribs.

His face gave nothing away.

"You can sit down," she said, surprised that her voice sounded almost normal.

He stepped toward her desk. "No thanks. I'll stand."

She inclined her head. "Okay."

He studied her, and she met his gaze, refusing to back down or be the first to speak. He'd sought her out. He could talk when he was ready. Maybe he was worried about her replacement, that they wouldn't give him the freedom that he'd had under her. Whatever. She wasn't going to make small talk just to put him at ease.

The seconds ticked by, and the underlying current she always felt when Ben was anywhere near her intensified. She struggled not to squirm in her chair.

"I'll go to Pennsylvania."

Her eyes widened. She stood, her hands on her desk, leaning forward. "Really?" she squeaked. She had been expecting it, but it still shocked her, somehow. He didn't look like a man who was giving in.

"Yeah. It shouldn't take more than six months to get that shop headed in the right direction." He jerked his head slightly, and for the first time, she noticed his knuckles were white as he gripped his hat. "But I have one condition."

"What's that?" she asked. He could tell her he wanted her to pack six moose and a rhinoceros and take them down with her, and she'd do it.

"While I'm there, you'll be my wife."

Chapter Nine

R iley blinked.

Her body stiffened like a hunk of meat in the freezer.

Ben looked completely serious. He wasn't smiling, and there didn't seem to be a punchline.

She'd dated.

Not a ton, since her heart and life were her work and she hadn't found a man who convinced her there was anything better.

Except Ben. When they'd been together, she'd felt like she would have given up everything to be with him. But in the end, she'd given him up instead.

But married?

She narrowed her eyes and tilted her head, picking up her pencil so her fingers had something to do. He seemed actually quite serious. "You want to marry me?"

"Not really," he said casually, and it felt like an insult. "But my gram is in the hospital, and my family thinks I'm married. The Coleman shop in Pennsylvania is right outside the town my family lives in. I'm not showing up down there without a wife."

So many questions bubbled around in her head. Why did his family think he was married? Why not tell them that he wasn't? Was he actually married? That one seemed important to her befuddled brain.

"You're not married to anyone else?"

His jaw muscles clenched, and a vein bulged in his neck. "Even an idiot like myself knows that's illegal."

She hadn't meant to insult him. Obviously he was sensitive about it, and she couldn't blame him. Not with their history. "I didn't mean it like that. I just don't understand why your family thinks you're married."

He shrugged it off. "It doesn't matter."

"You want to get married for real?"

"I'm not going to tell them you're my wife when you really aren't."

His jaw set in a stubborn line, like he expected her to challenge him. Silence descended.

She took a breath. "We could pretend..."

His eyes settled on her once again. "Married for real. That's my offer. Take it or leave it." There was a beat of silence, but before she could say anything, he added, "If you leave it, that's fine. Consider this my two-week notice."

The pencil point snapped. She pried her fingers off and set the pencil down deliberately. Ben was quitting?

Racking her brain for coherent thought, she said, "You can't just plan a wedding on the spur of the moment. I'd need at least six months."

He shook his head. "Won't work. I'm going to Pennsylvania this afternoon. We can go to the courthouse and get hitched first, or I'll go to PA alone. If I do, I'll see my family, then I'm heading to Montana to start my own business."

"But your two-week notice?"

"I'll be using personal days. And Paul has agreed to cover for me."

She'd allowed them the ability to do that on occasion. Obviously he was taking advantage of it now.

He stood in front of her, tall and dark and quiet. The idea of working without him had given her an empty feeling inside. She didn't work side by side with him, but in the summer, she saw him every day through the open garage door. She caught occasional glimpses of him on security cameras, which were attached to her computer, and during meetings and such.

They were a team, both of them pulling together. They'd been able to complement each other like no one else she'd ever been around.

But marry him?

Sure, there was this crazy attraction. But that wasn't enough to build a marriage on. Wait...

"You said you could have it headed in the right direction in six months."

"Yeah."

"What about after that?"

"If it needs more help, I'm not opposed to staying longer."

"So you'll only stay for six months or until it's performing at the top?"

"Yeah."

"Then what?"

"That's when I'll leave to start my own business."

"So you're leaving either way?"

"Yep."

"What about me? Our...marriage?"

A shadow flickered over his face, gone before she could examine it. "It's not going to be a real marriage. We'll get it annulled. I'm just not lying to my family while I'm there. Not any more than I have to." He paused, and the word "again" seemed to whisper in the air around them. "If I have a woman standing beside me and I say she's my wife, she's going to be my wife."

It was crazy. She shouldn't be considering it. Why was she even asking questions about it? But she knew. Because pleasing her dad and working for his company had been all she'd ever known.

Maybe she was also giving in to the pull that Ben had always exerted on her. Not that their "marriage" was going to mean anything. Of course, there was still the problem that existed all those years ago when she'd walked away from him the first time. This time, though, her dad wouldn't have anything to hold over her head. Nothing that would hurt Ben anyway.

Before she could use rational sense. Before she could chicken out. She straightened. "I'll do it."

~

RILEY PLACED her phone on speaker as she packed the last of the things she was taking from her office. It rang. And rang.

This was why she hardly ever called her mom. Her mom never answered. Seemed like she was always out doing something. She'd text later, apologizing for missing her call, saying she was out somewhere.

Had Riley called her mom even twice this year?

But marriage, even a fake one, was a big step, and Riley just felt like she needed to get her mother's opinion on it. Not permission. Not even acceptance. Her mother wouldn't know Ben. But she supposed there were certain times in a woman's life when she needed her mom. Marriage was one of those times. Even if it wasn't going to be real. Maybe especially if it wasn't going to be real.

Okay. Maybe she just wasn't sure that what she was doing was a great idea, and she needed to talk to someone. Someone who lived life to the fullest and wasn't afraid to take chances. She could hardly call friends she barely spoke to anymore for advice on a fake marriage.

Her mom's voicemail came on.

Riley swiped off, not even considering leaving a message. Disappointment swirled in her chest. A familiar feeling when she was dealing with her mother.

She tapped her finger on the edge of the box she'd filled with her personal items. Then she picked up her phone and found her dad's contact.

He picked up on the second ring. "What?"

"I just wanted to tell you I'd be in Pennsylvania tonight. I've already arranged housing at the business-owned farmhouse. I'll be in to work tomorrow."

"Good. I'll see that your office is ready. The woman you're replacing left last week."

"My replacement has been hired, and I'm taking over all employment decisions at the PA terminal."

"I'll make sure the staff understands," her dad said brusquely.

Her dad hated Ben. That's why she'd already taken care of his employment at the Brickley Springs terminal. It was something her dad would find out eventually, but that didn't need to be today. Hopefully it would be after they'd started getting the shop to perform.

She supposed moms and dads were different—she'd never really been around her mom much. Still, she wasn't tempted to tell her dad about her marriage at all. Most of that was probably because he'd blow a gasket if he found out she was going to marry Ben, but also because he just wouldn't be interested. The way she got his attention was by performing.

Maybe she thought her mom would be different. She should have known her mom wouldn't answer.

She drew her attention back to their conversation. "Thanks. That'll be helpful. I'll be able to hit the ground running."

"I wouldn't expect anything else."

"I haven't met my replacement. She's not arriving until Monday." Ben hadn't given her a choice about when she was leaving. She wanted to get moving, so she hadn't put up a fight about it. Or maybe she'd just been too shell-shocked about the fact that she'd actually agreed to get married. To Ben. "Audrey will handle everything."

"That's good. Hire yourself a secretary when you come down. Or two if you need. You know you have the freedom to make any and all changes you need."

"Thanks, Dad."

"Sure. Whatever it takes to pull this terminal up. I want it to be the top-performing shop when the investors show up. I gotta go." He hung up without saying goodbye.

Riley sighed, looking down at her phone. She'd never done anything that had garnered her mother's attention. But she knew what it took to impress her dad. She looked at the box and squared her shoulders. Maybe she was crazy, but getting married to someone she barely knew wasn't too much to do if it meant she'd succeed in her dad's eyes.

Although she had to admit she wouldn't have married just anyone. Ben had always been different than other men to her. She knew she could trust him, and she knew he had what it took to turn the terminal around.

She was just putting the last of her things into the final box when Eve pushed her office door open and looked around. "Good morning, Riley. I know you're probably busy, but do you have a minute?"

"I sure do. Come on in." She was packed and ready to go. She'd had a moving company come to her apartment earlier in the week, taking some things to storage and some to Pennsylvania. She just had a few suitcases. "Actually, I was just finishing up here, and I'm glad for something to pass the time."

Eve stepped in.

"Come on in and sit down." Riley indicated two comfortable chairs in the corner of her office that angled toward each other. "These are pretty comfortable. I'm going to miss them."

Eve smiled. "Ben's already been in to see you?"

"Yes." Riley gave her a direct look.

"And you said?"

"I agreed."

Something that looked like relief went over Eve's face. Then she looked at her lap, turning her phone over and over in her hands, like an alligator death roll. She looked very young when she finally lifted her head and spoke. "I want to ask a question, but it's personal."

Riley kept her expression clear, although a little chill ran down her spine. "Okay."

"You don't have to answer." She gave a half-smile.

The chill reached out and wrapped around her ribs. "Okay."

"Something happened between you and Ben a long time ago. Eden and I have figured that much out. But Ben won't talk. Will you tell me?"

Riley blew a breath out. She hesitated because it was really Ben's story to tell. Riley was the bad guy. But maybe Ben hadn't wanted to talk bad about her. She could see Ben holding it in because of that; really, she could.

So, it would fall to her to tell the story. But the twins might hate her, and she liked Eden and Eve a lot. She walked to the coffee maker that she was leaving for the next occupant and poured herself a cup. "Would you like some?"

"No. Thank you."

Riley held the cup in her hand and started toward her chair. "I don't want you to hate me."

"I won't. I promise."

She smiled. "You'll think less of me. I know. But I guess I deserve it." She took a sip of her coffee then realized she hadn't put any cream or sugar in it. "Ugh." She got back up. "Back when we were in high school, well, even before that. I think Ben was around fourteen when he moved up to Maine."

"He actually ran away from his home." Eve stated it like it was a fact everyone knew.

Riley poured the creamer in her coffee. "I didn't know that until recently." Her heart clenched. She stood still, picturing Ben, determined and angry, making his way to his mother. Yes. She could see it. Nothing could have stopped him from going to be with her once he found out about her. Even at fourteen. Her heart pinched for the boy he'd been. "I just knew he showed up in school about ninth grade. He was gorgeous."

"He still is," Eden said.

"True." Riley giggled. "I guess I'm getting married to him. I can admit that, right?"

Eden laughed. "I won't tell him you said so."

"He knows it."

"Actually, I don't think he does."

Riley couldn't imagine he didn't. "Anyway, we had a class together, and when he learned that my dad owned a trucking company, he asked me if I could get him permission to hang around the garage." She shrugged. "So I did."

They'd talked in class some and met once behind the bleachers, she couldn't even remember what for...maybe for her to return the hat he'd left in class or something. Something innocent.

But after that first time, they'd just kind of shown up there every morning, and for twenty minutes or so, they'd talked.

Completely innocent. He'd never kissed her. It wasn't like they made out behind the bleachers. Nothing like that. But one morning that spring, he'd asked her to go to the prom with him.

She'd said yes. With fireworks shooting out of her heart and her entire being thrilled that the boy she was falling for had asked her out.

They never walked the halls together. Except for that one history class, they were in completely different rooms and tracks. They'd never "gone steady" or any of the other things that her friends did. Ben was different. It was part of his attraction.

"And he learned mechanical stuff from being around the mechanics at Coleman?" Eve asked, interrupting her thoughts.

"Yes. He did. It was the best thing he could have done."

"And you helped him. How does that make you look bad?"

"Oh, our story doesn't end there." If only.

"No?" She sat a little straighter on the chair. "Keep going."

Riley tapped her cup. "So, your mom had you two, and also Ben, and of course, your dad didn't do much in the way of support."

"I know Ben said Mom didn't want to rock the boat and endanger Eden and me, so she didn't insist on child support."

Riley nodded. "I think that's the way lots of women feel."

"What was she like?" Eve asked softly.

Riley barely remembered Ben's mother. "She was beautiful. Gentle. Quiet. I remember her as a real lady."

"You didn't have a mom?" Eve wrinkled her nose.

"Not really. I mean, I do. She's with her fifth husband and living in the Bahamas. She didn't want me." Riley took a drink of coffee to disguise the hurt in her heart.

"That's sad."

"Yeah. Anyway." It was ancient history, and she just had to deal with it. "When her lupus started getting worse, Ben was beside himself. He was fifteen, and he wanted to work, to help provide since your mother had to quit her job—she was a waitress. But he was too young."

"And?"

"So, I told you, I helped him get a job. Dad was already grooming me to work in his business. From the time I could walk, I followed him around the company. I knew the ins and outs—I'd worked there every summer since I could read. Anyway, I...falsified Ben's birth certificate, made him older than he was, and I made sure he got hired for second shift. Back then, the Maine terminal was our only terminal. It wasn't until I graduated from high school that Dad expanded and moved and Pennsylvania became our home base."

"So Ben was able to go to school and also work." Eve pushed her hair back behind her ear. Her face was still open and friendly. They hadn't gotten to the bad part of the story yet.

"Yep."

"No one found out?"

"People knew. But they also knew the situation with your mom and that she couldn't work and she had you two…"

"No one said anything." Eve looked thoughtful.

"Nope."

She shrugged. "I still don't see how you're the bad guy."

Riley swallowed. "It's coming. Trust me."

"Okay."

"Like I said, people knew, but Ben was good at what he did. It wasn't long until he had to turn down a promotion to day shift, even. But your mom got worse."

"She died." Eve said it matter-of-factly with a lifted shoulder. Riley supposed it was just a fact of life to her. She'd been very young when it happened.

"Eventually. But Ben and I…" How did she explain what they were? Friends, yeah, kind of. "We didn't really date, but we liked each other. I knew he liked me, and I really liked him." She smiled. She had really, *really* liked him. "But Ben had a lot of responsibility on his shoulders, and he was working all the time, and you don't really know my dad, but he had plans for me that didn't include me getting mixed up with a mechanic from the shop. And I knew that."

Eve's brows drew down. "Ben wasn't good enough for him?"

"Yeah. That's basically it." And nothing had changed. At all.

"Ben asked me to go to prom with him, and I said yes. He was coming to my house to pick me up. But my dad found out…I think it was the day before. He got one of his business friends to have their son come take me." She fingered her cup. She couldn't even remember the boy's name. He'd just finished his second year of college, and her dad thought pretty highly of him.

"My dad was furious that I'd been kind of seeing Ben, a mechanic. I didn't usually buck him, but I was a little defiant about Ben." She'd really, really liked him. "I was a teenager, and I was all like, 'but I love him, Daddy.' But Dad said if I ever spoke to him again, Dad would make sure he got fired and never worked for Coleman Trucking again. Furthermore, he said he would make sure that he never worked as a mechanic again." She'd believed him at the time. "Looking back, I don't know if he could have done that. But I do know that Ben needed that job. His mother was dying, and he had twin sisters to raise, and his dad was a deadbeat. I was scared that Ben would lose you two, and I knew he'd be devastated over that."

Eve nodded. She knew what was at stake for Ben.

"Dad made sure that I understood that the break needed to be permanent. I wasn't to string him along or have him come to me asking if I'd change my mind or anything. Dad promised that he would keep his job. He promised that he'd even get a pay raise, but I could never have contact with him again. First time he caught Ben trying to talk to me, even if I didn't answer him, he was terminated."

Eve's eyes got big, and her knuckles whitened as she held her phone. "Wow. That's harsh."

"I know he probably was trying to protect me and trying to do what was best for me." Actually she really wasn't sure, but she hoped it was true.

"Maybe."

Riley shrugged. It didn't make any difference at this point in time. "Dad insisted I go to the dance with that other boy. He insisted that I walk out the door on his arm, with all of my friends and their dates behind me. Man, there must have been twenty of us..." Her voice trailed off.

She could still see Ben standing there, unable to afford to rent a tux, but looking better than anyone she'd ever seen in clean jeans and a nice white collared shirt. A bouquet of grocery store flowers in his hand. It'd been the hardest thing she'd ever done in her life to stop, with her hand holding onto the arm of another boy, and tell Ben all the things her dad had told her to. But when they'd met in the mornings, he'd talked with pride, affection, and deep love about his twin sisters and the promises he'd made to his mother to take care of them. She couldn't be the reason he'd lost it all.

It was one of the hardest things she'd ever done. "I told Ben he was a fool for thinking that I might actually go somewhere in public with him." She took a breath. "I said he wasn't good enough for me and never would be. I called him white trash and a scum ball and a bunch of other insults."

"He stood there?"

"Yeah. He stood there. My dad stood at the door, smiling. My friends laughed behind me. I smiled back at my dad, so Ben would know that he wasn't making me do it."

"Wow. That was harsh." Eve repeated her earlier phrase, only with more heat this time. Her eyes narrowed at Riley.

Riley figured she wouldn't be her favorite person in the world after she confessed what a horrible person she'd been. "It was." It was so very harsh. "But it worked. Ben is still working for our company."

"So when did you tell Ben that your dad made you do it?"

"I never did."

"What?" Eve almost jumped out of her chair.

"What's the point?"

"So that he'd know you didn't really mean it? That you didn't think he was worthless? That you did what you did because you truly cared for him?" Eve's eyes were big, her cheeks red.

Riley looked away. How could she? So much time had passed. She'd actually thought about it when she first came back from college and they worked here together. But they hardly ever saw one another, and days slipped into weeks and years. She'd been tempted to just confront him, but he was still caring for the twins and she was still trying to please her dad and move up in the company. Whatever they'd had in high school was long over. There'd always been an attraction to Ben, but soon she became his boss, so it didn't matter anyway. Did it? She couldn't change it.

As though Eve realized where her thoughts were headed, she said, "It's not what you did, it's that you never told him any different. Once he was no longer in danger of losing his job..."

"That's just it. You two just started making your own money and working for yourselves. Up until this very point in time, me being seen with Ben could have caused him to lose everything he'd worked for. It still could."

"Do you really think your dad would still fire Ben? Does he really hate him that much?"

"It's not about hating him. Dad doesn't hate him. It's more about controlling me, I think. Dad wants me to end up with someone who will sit at the head of the corporate meeting table and take over the reins from him. Not someone with grease on his hands and no college diploma in his pocket."

"It's so hard to believe that your dad would be that awful." Eve leaned back in her chair, rubbing her chin. Finally, she asked hesitantly, "Do you still have feelings for Ben?"

Riley hesitated. "I like him. Of course I do. I admire him too. Who else would have sacrificed what he has to raise his sisters alone?"

"I think you deliberately misunderstood me."

Riley took a big gulp of her coffee and searched her brain for something to change the subject with.

But Eve wouldn't let it go. "There was a spark there once. Do you think you could love my brother?"

Riley couldn't be anything but honest. "I think it'd be easy to love your brother." She would never have agreed to enter into a fake marriage with just anyone. The idea of being "fake" married to any other guy she knew was repulsive. "But I think you can tell from my story that the real question is could your brother possibly love me. Especially after what I've done to him. The things I told you that I said and did, I really said and did them. How could he ever forgive or forget?"

Eve's lips flattened.

"And you had a good point. Surely, at some time, I could have, should have, gone to him and admitted what I did. I could have gone behind my dad's back or even risked getting Ben fired. But even though it was something I wanted to do, I never did. And yes, I didn't want Ben to lose his job when he was supporting you two, but I know there's also a part of me that doesn't want to disappoint my dad." She felt it long and strong every time her dad wanted her to do something for him. She'd work herself to death to make him happy.

"I've worked hard for what I have, even though my dad is the owner. But also, my whole life has been making choices that make Dad happy." Riley studied Eden. "You don't want to disappoint Ben."

"No." A little light dawned in her eyes. "That's true."

"Don't forget, my mom didn't want me. She left and didn't even bother to take her daughter with her. That's not something a girl forgets. And I'm sure it's affected how much I crave my dad's approval, since getting my mom's love was never an option." Even as the words left her mouth, she knew they were true. It was why she'd stood on the step all those years ago and did exactly what her dad wanted.

Eve nodded. "I hate how complicated everything is. Eden and I were holding out hope that you and Ben would fall in love and stay together. You're great for him, and we've always kind of felt like he has feelings for you."

Did he? How could she not see that?

"I don't know about that, but I do know that he could have feelings and still not trust me. Or even like me."

"At the very least, I think you should tell Ben why you dumped him and in such a mean way. It's only fair that he know it wasn't him, and it wasn't because he wasn't good enough."

Eve was right, of course. And she'd tried. It had never worked. Now, it was done and over with, and he wasn't interested in going back. She had to let it go.

Chapter Ten

Ben was still somewhat in shock as he drove his pickup to the courthouse. He hadn't expected Riley to say yes. Not really. He'd made his demands as unreasonable as possible. That she do it today. That they leave for Pennsylvania this afternoon. That he was only in for six months.

That last didn't sit well. He didn't know what kind of vows he'd be saying in a few minutes, but he'd never given his word lightly. It hardly seemed right to start now, entering into the most sacred of God's covenants with man.

Unfortunately he'd not thought of that earlier. He'd been too eager to exact his version of revenge.

He hadn't been to too many weddings, but he was pretty sure there were some promises to love and cherish for as long as they both lived.

Man, he hated to say he'd do it and all the while be planning on not. Cold feet.

That's what his doubts were called. Right?

Riley sat beside him, her hands in her lap, staring out the window. He could admit that he'd dreamed more than once about Riley being beside him, not just in his pickup but anywhere. But in his dreams, there had never been this strained silence between them. Nor was there this almost animosity. The underlying buzz of attraction, yeah. Definitely that was the same. But in his dreams, she liked him.

He pulled into the courthouse parking lot. The lowered clouds and dark sky reflected the mood in the truck.

He wouldn't want Eve's or Eden's wedding day to be like this. Even if it were a fake marriage. His sisters had better not have a fake marriage.

He pulled into a parking space and turned to Riley. "You know, you don't have to do this."

She turned, her heart-shaped chin lifted in challenge. "Cold feet?"

Heck, yeah.

"I don't want to do this and have you hate me."

Her surprise was real. "Why would I hate you? You're doing me a favor."

"You haven't said a word on the drive here." With the twins, if they weren't talking, that meant they were mad. Always his fault.

"Neither have you."

The twins never noticed if he wasn't talking. Not usually, anyway.

"I was thinking," he said, not liking the defensive tone that crept into his voice.

"Me too." She lifted a brow in challenge. "Happy thoughts about how we're going to turn the world upside down in Pennsylvania."

"Confident much?"

"I've got *you*."

He caught his breath. His heart stumbled. She was that confident in him? She wanted him to help her so badly she was willing to marry him, when she didn't even like him, in order to do it? Marry him with only a few hours' notice and move eight hours away.

Something in his chest expanded, low and deep. She really believed in him. Once, a long time ago, she might have tossed his love in the trash like yesterday's leftovers, but she really did believe in him.

"Don't worry," she said. "I'll make sure your family thinks we've been married for...how long?"

"Four years." That would cover the lie he'd told Gram.

"Four years. And we...don't want kids?"

He paused in the act of reaching for the door latch, looking over at Riley. There was no hidden meaning in her words, but they'd struck something inside of him. Would their kids have her hazel eyes that changed with her moods? His dark hair? Her delicate bone structure? Her easy smile? His attention to detail? Her stubborn determination? Oh, God help them if anyone's children were as stubbornly determined as Riley was to earn her spot at the top of her dad's company.

He shrugged, looking away, not wanting to say anything that would make this day any worse than what it already was. "I guess not. We don't have any."

She laughed a little at that. Just something more than a snort, but it froze him again.

Her laughter. It hit him deep inside, in that spot that felt warm. It pulsed there, spreading quiet joy throughout his whole body. His fingertips tingled. He wanted to hear it again. Wanted to see her smile. For goodness' sake, it was her wedding day.

It wasn't real.

He turned and yanked the door latch. "Let's get this over with."

RILEY WALKED to the steps of the courthouse, very conscious of the large man beside her. He seemed fine—just another day for him. On the other hand, her internal organs had staged a revolt, and her heart was snapping the whip behind them.

On the top step, Ben touched her arm. "Hang on."

He turned and jogged back down the stairs, crossing the street and getting in the glovebox of his pickup. He held a small package in his hand as he came back up the stairs.

Her face crinkled.

"A ring," he said simply. She nodded.

She'd been in the courthouse once or twice before for jury duty, so the metal detectors and the serious-faced, uniformed guard at the entrance were not a surprise. Today, though, she didn't enjoy the ornate molding and the huge, high ceilings. Didn't admire the intricate carved woodwork of a century past when a man actually made his living making beautiful things out of native lumber for the sole purpose of making the inside of a living area look resplendent and classy. Normally she loved admiring the handiwork of generations ago, even if it had nothing at all to do with her and the job she did.

But today, as she walked down the expansive hall, every little noise echoing against the walls, she wondered how many other couples had taken this same walk. The courthouse seemed to be the place to go if your marriage wasn't exactly a love match. Ben and she were not the first to walk these halls, six inches of space between them, not talking, not even planning on taking their vows seriously or keeping them.

Her hand accidentally brushed his, and he jerked it away. She pretended not to notice even as her heart contracted. What was she getting into? She was marrying a man who, if he didn't hate her, at least loathed her, and for good reason.

She felt like she was walking through a cloud as they showed their ID to the bored-looking lady at the desk and signed the proper papers.

The woman didn't even look up as she said, "Sit down over there. I'll call you when the judge can take five minutes."

Five minutes.

An annoyance for the judge.

A life change for her.

Blindly she followed Ben to the hard wooden chairs along the wall. These were probably hand-carved, too, and on any other day, she would have admired the workmanship.

Ben sat with legs apart and leaned his forearms on his knees. She lowered herself primly beside him, crossing her legs and resisting the urge to pull her phone out. She couldn't handle reading the news headlines right now, but a game where she got to shoot lots of things might be good stress relief.

Gripping her purse with fingers that wanted to shake, she stared at the wall and concentrated on taking deep, relaxing breaths. Ben might not like her, but he wasn't a monster. He was a good man, and in return for her suffering through this, he was going to make the shop in Brickley Springs profitable again.

His hands were folded in front of him, and he looked as relaxed as a man who had nothing more on his mind than thinking about the contents of his toolbox.

She wished it were that easy for her.

Finally, the woman at the desk called them and directed them back through big, heavy wooden doors. Ben opened one and held it for her.

"Thank you," she murmured.

He grunted.

A man with thinning gray hair, apparently the judge, stood behind his desk. He wore a white dress shirt with no tie and a pair of dress pants. No robe.

He came around the desk with a small book in his hand. He held his other hand out to them. "I'm Judge Croker. You two are here to get married?"

His smile revealed straight, white teeth.

"Yes, sir," Ben answered as Riley nodded. She made sure her handshake was firm and confident, and she reached deep inside for the fake confidence she always used with her dad. Maybe it was a mistake, but she wasn't going to make herself sick thinking about it. The decision had been made. Now she was going to jump headfirst in.

The judge looked between the two of them, like he was looking for some sign that showed they actually wanted what they said they wanted. Ben's expression didn't change. He stood solid and strong beside her. She lifted her chin a fraction of an inch and met the judge's eyes with a small smile.

"Okay, well, we'll get started then. Face each other and clasp right hands."

It took Riley three seconds to figure out which hand was her right. She clasped Ben's waiting hand.

A small shock went through her. His hand was rough and hard. Big. Strong. Their eyes met for a fraction of a second as invisible currents of something hot and prickly shot between them. For the first time since he'd made his offer, Ben's face showed something besides complete control. It was just a widening of his eyes, a twitch of his lips, but she was sure whatever shock she felt, he'd felt it too.

It wasn't her imagination, either, that the hold of his hand lightened, and cool air seeped between their hands. He seemed to be holding it with two fingers, like he'd hold a pail of garbage that he didn't really want to touch. She tried not to be offended.

The judge's words flowed past her, and she responded at the proper time, not really paying attention until he asked for a ring.

Ben reached into his front pocket and pulled out a small package of O-rings. Riley's eyes widened slightly as he broke the little bag and pulled out one of the rubber rings.

The judge, who had probably thought he'd seen it all, stood with his mouth slightly open, watching Ben's hands as he slid the black band onto her left hand.

Judge Croker shook his head slightly and continued with the vows.

Riley supposed it was a good thing she hadn't been able to get a hold of her mother. If her mother asked her anything, anything at all, she'd want to know about the size of her ring.

She fingered the odd-feeling rubber band as the judge pronounced them man and wife. Rather than telling Ben to kiss his bride, he turned to his desk and pointed to the paper on it. "Sign this."

It stated they were married. Until death do them part. She supposed it should have said, *Until the Coleman Trucking terminal is running in the black at the top of the company again*, but there wasn't enough room. It didn't really have a good ring to it anyway.

She signed and watched as Ben picked up the pen in his capable fingers and drew his bold signature over the correct line.

And that was it.

They walked out, married, and she tried not to be upset because it seemed like just another day at the office to everyone else in the courthouse.

Just because it was special to her...

She pushed that thought away. It was a fake marriage. It shouldn't be special.

They walked out to the pickup. Ben opened her door without saying anything then closed it behind her and got in on his side.

They'd already loaded the stuff from her apartment, so they were ready to take off for Brickley Springs.

"You hungry?" Ben's voice broke into her thoughts. Deep and clear. Confident. It was a voice that soothed her and gave her courage.

"Not really." She hadn't had an appetite since he'd made his suggestion this morning. At one time, she'd dreamed of marrying him. Never like this.

"I'm going to stop for fast food then." He turned toward her. "I'll take you somewhere nice, though, if you want." He looked back out the windshield at the town streets. "I know it's not real, but it was your first marriage, and it's not every day that a girl gets married. Plus," his fingers did a slow tap on the steering wheel, "we need to get used to the idea that we have to look real." He slowed for a red light. "Anyway, I'll take you out if you want."

It was on the tip of her tongue to say that she made more money than he did and if anyone were taking anyone out, it would be her paying for his meal, but she shut her mouth hard. Ben looked confident and almost invincible, but he had a lot of pride, and a man's pride was easily bruised. She'd taken that pride and smashed it once. She wasn't making that mistake again. Not if she could help it.

"Thanks for the offer." She appreciated the consideration. "I'm really not hungry."

His lips flattened, and he pulled toward the nearest drive-thru.

She looked out the window, unsure what she'd done that had made him look so irritated with her.

He ordered and ate while he drove. The time and distance slipped by. She allowed herself a little bit of time to adjust, time to be sorry that her "wedding day" hadn't even come close to what she'd dreamed of.

But after an hour or so, she'd done enough wallowing. They needed to face the future, and they needed a plan. "I helped raise the twins, right?"

"For the last four years, I guess you did."

She half expected him to not answer, so she was surprised when he shifted in his seat, glancing over, his dark sunglasses and beard stubble making him look rugged and handsome. Her heart swished in her chest. For now, he was hers. The thought made her smile. She liked the idea that this rugged, capable man belonged to her. "I didn't give you a ring."

"I couldn't wear one anyway. Not in the shop. I'd lose my finger."

"Oh." She looked back out the window. There was so much she didn't know. Not just about him but about what he did, despite the fact that she worked in the same company and her dad owned it. Maybe she'd never know. "I'm surprised the twins weren't at our wedding. Aren't they going to Pennsylvania too?"

"It wasn't real. There wasn't any reason for them to be there." He tapped the steering wheel again. "They're coming down. But I guess they needed more than a couple of hours to pack."

"They're going to close up the house?"

"Kind of. I'll need to go back up for my toolbox."

"Couldn't you just put it in the back?" She looked over her shoulder. There was plenty of room in the bed of his pickup.

He snorted. "No way. I might even hire someone to bring it down."

"It's that special?"

"Yeah."

He didn't elaborate, and she didn't ask any more questions. They should know more about each other, but he didn't seem interested in knowing anything about her, and she was tired. She leaned her head against the window and fell asleep.

Chapter Eleven

Ben listened to the woman beside him snore. She'd been out for the past several hours, and now that they were less than thirty minutes from the hospital where his gram was, he figured he should wake her. But how?

If it were one of the twins, he'd just grab her arm and shake her. He hadn't coddled them growing up. Maybe they could have used the softness of a mother's touch at times, but they had each other to comfort themselves, so he hadn't worried about it.

But Riley? It seemed a little calloused to just grab her and shake.

Not to mention, he'd touched her at the courthouse. Just her hand, but it had almost been a disastrous mistake. Whatever the attraction was that constantly simmered inside of him when she was around had exploded into bright lights and shooting sparks when he'd gripped her hand. Maybe it was the nervousness combined with the atmosphere—they were getting married after all—but he'd have dropped her hand like a hot iron if he could have. As it was, he'd held as lightly as he could with two fingers, hoping she didn't notice.

He glanced over again.

Her snoring was kind of cute. He'd never have thought that she'd snore. Guess the amount of money your family had didn't affect what you did while you were sleeping.

What had he done?

Actually, what had she done? She should have had him sign a prenup. One that was about three thousand pages long to keep him from getting any of her family's precious money or assets. He must have really surprised her to keep her from even suggesting it.

He would have signed. He wasn't after her stuff.

Maybe she trusted him.

He already knew she believed in him. Did she trust him that much, too? It wasn't like she didn't know him. Or at least know his reputation.

The sun had set long ago, and as he slowed to make a turn, the streetlights hit her face, soft and vulnerable in slumber. Light lashes resting on soft cheeks. Her slender hands tucked under her chin.

He always thought of her as strong and decisive. Determined. But right now, she looked fragile and defenseless. It stirred his protective instincts. Like the twins did. Like when his mother had gotten sick. He wanted to reach over and draw her closer, pull her into the protected circle of his arm. Have her rest her head on his shoulder and lean on him. After all, she believed in him, and she trusted him too. The least he could do was protect her.

He'd married her. Real or fake, he considered it his job to take care of this woman.

There would be time later to consider the implications of that. Riley probably didn't want his protection or care, although that's really all he had to offer in exchange for her belief in him and her trust. Didn't really seem like a fair exchange when he'd take all she was giving but she didn't want all he had to offer. He shook those thoughts away.

Thankfully she stirred when he pulled into the hospital parking lot. It was nearly empty, and he found a spot while she straightened and looked around. "We're here?"

"Yeah."

He pulled out his phone, more to give her some time to wake up than because he thought he missed anything. There was a text from Cassidy's number telling him Gram had asked about him and another saying they were leaving the hospital for the day because visiting hours were over.

Well, he might be able to intimidate the nurses into letting him see his gram, but he'd put money on Riley being able to sweet-talk them into it. He grinned. It was nice to have that kind of competence on his side.

He looked over at her. "Visiting hours were over forty-five minutes ago. Think you can get us in to see Gram?"

The sleepy look had faded from her eyes, but a piece of her hair was bent over the wrong way. He reached up to move it.

Her mouth had opened, maybe to answer him, but she froze as his hand touched her hair. He smoothed it down, marveling. With the twins, he'd kept their hair short until they could do it themselves, even though he loved long hair. It was too much trouble to mess with, with everything else he had to do. But with his fingers on Riley's hair? His breath slowed way down as the silk slid along his fingertips, and he actually had to grit his teeth against the desire to plunge his fingers into it, every cell in his hand wanting to feel it slide along his rougher skin.

Her eyes widened, maybe at the look on his face, and he dropped his hand immediately.

"I can probably get us in." Her voice sounded weak, like a motor with no turbo. "Do you know where we're going?"

"Yeah, I've got the room number." His heart rate had gone back to almost normal, although his voice held a rough note that wasn't usually there. "You ready?"

She jerked her chin up and reached for the door handle.

He should be opening the door for her. Why not?

"Wait." He got out and walked around.

One side of her lips turned up as he opened her door and offered his hand. "There's no one watching. You don't have to do this."

"I've never been any good at pretending to be something some of the time, just to impress someone who's watching. You're my wife. I want to open your door."

He couldn't read her expression. Her gaze was on their hands. Hers white and soft. His dark and rough. The contrast was obvious and striking. It made him want to protect her even more, until he realized what she was probably thinking.

She'd said he wasn't good enough. Their hands told the whole story. A person couldn't look at his hands and not know with certainty that he did manual labor for a living. Hers? They looked like a pampered millionaire's hands. Too good for the likes of him. Especially when one took in the ring on her finger. It looked crude and ugly next to the porcelain white smoothness of her perfect skin.

He helped her out and closed her door, slamming it a little harder than necessary.

He'd been right. It didn't take Riley fifteen seconds to convince the nurses to allow them to go back to his gram's room, and suddenly, he was walking in to see the grandmother he hadn't seen in twenty years, almost to the day.

Very conscious of the woman beside him, of the unresolved animosity between them, and especially of the fact that they were supposed to be happily married, he walked down the hall, close but not touching.

He intended to do everything humanly possible to help her get her company's terminal running in the black, cash in at the top of the company, make her dad proud, and get the corner office that he knew she coveted. He would insist that she play the part of his wife with equal dedication.

Which meant he was going to take her hand.

Would she allow it?

It would be better to find out here in the hall, out of sight of his grandmother and family members.

Married couples didn't necessarily need to hold hands, a little voice in his head said quite clearly. He knew it was right. He didn't want to take her hand because of his gram. He wanted to take her hand because walking beside her this close and not touching her was torture.

But she looked down on him. She didn't think he was good enough. She couldn't have been more clear when she'd said that to him in high school.

His heart hardened, and his jaw set.

Then her hand touched his. His breath caught. He wavered for a millisecond before he took her hand, threading their fingers together. He'd never kissed her, but he'd held her hand when they met behind the bleachers before school, every morning of their senior year from Christmas until the night of prom.

He pushed the thought away, unwilling to remember.

The sparks were still there. Muted. Her hand felt like it was made for his, perfectly fitting as skin slid against skin. His arm tingled, and his heart warmed.

Riley must have felt his unease, because she squeezed his hand. He squeezed back, wanting to pull her closer, not wanting to let go. The thought scared him a little. The marriage was for convenience and revenge. Why was he enjoying holding her hand and squeezing it? He almost pulled his hand away but stopped himself. He didn't need to remove his hand. He simply had to stop enjoying holding hers. Easier said than done.

He squared his shoulders and stepped in as Riley thanked the nurse.

An old woman, so much older than the picture in his mind, lay on the hospital bed, hooked up to lines and monitors. White hair billowed in a thin cloud around her head. Same stubborn chin. Wrinkles where her smile lines were.

No fear and no uncertainty in her frail body. Maybe she hadn't changed that much.

A thin curtain separated her from her roommate whose TV flashed in the dim lighting. At least it wasn't blaring loud.

His gram's eyes were open. They narrowed. Recognition flashed.

"Jimmy?" she said.

He cringed. She thought he was his dad. Grateful for Riley—at least he could prove that he hadn't deserted his "wife" like his dad—he stepped closer. "It's Ben."

"Benjamin?" His gram's blue eyes lit up. "Is that you?"

Something buzzed against his side. Riley's hand slipped out of his, and she pulled her phone out. He could read the screen: DAD.

She looked up at him. "I need to get this."

He tilted his chin. She'd done what she needed to do for him. Gram had seen her at least.

Riley turned and stepped out into the hallway. For a brief moment,

Ben wondered if that's the way it would be if they were married for real. Daddy first. If Riley had a flaw, that was it.

He turned back to his gram. She struggled to sit.

"No, Gram. Stay down. You remember me? Ben?"

"Cassidy whispered to me that you were coming."

"Told her I would."

"I didn't believe it," she rasped. "It's been twenty years since you left."

"Long time."

She looked back past his shoulder, her eyes hopeful. "Was that one of your sisters?"

"No."

Her shoulders stooped.

He took a breath. He didn't have to lie. Not about this, at least. "That was my wife. Riley." It felt good to be able to tell the truth, and he made a mental note to thank Riley. He didn't think he'd done that. Of course, he was going to work his heart out for her, just so she could put a smile on her old man's face. That should be thanks enough.

"Riley? I don't think you ever told me her name."

"Probably not." He looked over his shoulder. Riley stood out in the hall, the phone to her ear. She wasn't talking. He smiled to himself. Probably she didn't do much talking when she was on the phone with her dad.

"She was pretty."

"Yeah." He supposed she was pretty. It wasn't something he'd ever really thought about. Her drive and commitment, her fearless tendency to jump in and figure things out as she went along, unafraid to admit she was wrong and change course, those were all things he'd admired in her since the first time he'd met her.

"Where are your sisters?" Gram's bony, wrinkled hand fingered the scratchy hospital sheets.

He stepped closer, until he was beside her, and reached down, picking up her hand and holding it. "They're coming tomorrow."

"Both of them?"

"Yes."

She squeezed his hand. "I never got to apologize for the way you found out about your mother and sisters." The machine above her clicked and rattled. The numbers flashed. Gram's eyes closed tiredly.

Compassion stirred in Ben's chest. "I realize now it wasn't your fault." His dad had been a real piece of work. He'd had two "wives" and had taken Ben from his mother and moved him in with his other wife so all his boys could be together. Ben had been too young to remember much, just had some nagging, ragged memories. His brothers' mother had been a nice woman. Duped just like his own mother.

"Fourteen-year-olds aren't the most rational age group on the planet." He tilted his head. "I'm sorry I ran away. I guess I could have talked to you, but you knew the truth all that time and never said anything."

His gram nodded sadly. "Your real mother was too afraid to say anything to anyone." Her hand shook in his. He used his other hand to stroke the top of it. "Your dad threatened to kidnap or hurt you if she called the police. She knew she was right, but she also knew he'd do what he said. He promised you'd be safe and cared for if she let you go." Her ice-blue eyes met his. "You were. I kept in touch with her. She wasn't a strong woman, and she didn't have any money or resources. I kept my mouth shut to keep the peace, too, although in hindsight, maybe I shouldn't have."

He nodded. The memories he had of his dad weren't good ones. But the man was this woman's son, and he wasn't going to bad-mouth him. "I shouldn't have opened that letter, but when I realized I had sisters, and that Dad hauled logs out of Maine so he could visit his other wife, my real mother, I couldn't stay any longer."

His real mother had found out about his dad's second family and written a letter telling him she knew. Ben had gotten the mail on his way in the door from school, and although he'd known it was wrong, he couldn't resist opening the letter addressed to his dad with a return address of "Pat Baxter." He might not have figured it out if she hadn't mentioned her son, Ben, and begged his dad to bring him home. Ten years after his dad had taken him, his mother still loved him, remembered him, and wanted him back.

"How did you get to Maine?" his gram asked, her voice soft and scratchy.

"Hitchhiked."

Her lips pressed together, and her face scrunched up like his answer hurt. It probably did. He'd die if his sisters decided to hitchhike from here to Maine.

"Thank God you made it."

"Yeah." He didn't want to talk about it, really. At the time, he'd been so angry at everyone. His mother, for not fighting for him. His gram, for knowing the truth and not telling him. His brothers because they got to live with their real mother, even if she was dying of cancer. But most of all, his dad. Which he figured he'd turned into a good thing, with his determination to not be like him. Not even a little.

Gram studied him, and he looked away, not really wanting her to see all the ugliness that he'd carried for a long time. A lot of anger.

His eyes landed on Riley at the foot of the bed. He hadn't realized she'd come back in. Her eyes held sorrow. But he thought he might have seen some admiration there, too. Although what she'd found to admire in that mess, he really didn't know.

She walked around and stood at his side. Awkwardness seemed to sit in the space between Riley and him, and it sure felt like his gram could see it. Those eyes might be old, but they were sharp.

It took him about five seconds of fighting with himself to not touch her before he decided he could put his arm around Riley. So he did. She leaned into him a little, and he lowered his head, breathing deep of her feminine scent. He couldn't place the scent, but it reminded him of ambition and determination and butterflies and steel wrapped in silk. And she believed in him.

"It's nice to finally meet you, Riley," his gram said.

Riley slipped out from under his arm and bent over the bed, hugging his gram. When she straightened, his gram had a look of peace on her face.

"I worried about you, Ben," Gram finally said. "Lean down here and give this old woman a hug."

Ben obeyed. He should have done it to begin with.

It was kind of funny that the pride that swelled in his chest should be for a wife that wasn't really a wife. But she'd made his gram happy and at peace. He definitely needed to thank her.

"It's late, and we told the nurse we wouldn't be long, so we'd better leave." He stepped back, thinking to reach for Riley's hand again. Strange how natural it felt to hold it. But he shoved his hand in his pocket instead. He didn't want to feel too at ease with her. There needed to be distance.

His gram closed her eyes. "Will I see you again? Or are you leaving for another twenty years?"

"I'm staying for a while. I'll be in tomorrow. Sometime." They hadn't talked about when they were starting at the Coleman terminal. They'd seen his gram. He felt Riley had been very convincing in her role as his wife. Ben was eager to get started keeping his end of their bargain. "The twins will be in, too."

"You're going to talk to your brothers?"

"My half brothers," he corrected. "I'd imagine we'll run into each other here at some point." He wasn't going to avoid them.

"You're the oldest. You're also the one who left."

For good reasons. But they'd done a good job of making his gram happy; he wasn't going to ruin that. "I hear ya. I'll think about it." He leaned down and kissed her dry forehead.

"It was good to meet you," Riley said.

His gram nodded and smiled without opening her eyes. "Take care of that boy. He looks like a tough one, but them's the ones that always have the soft insides."

Riley slanted her eyes at him. Her thoughtful look made him uncomfortable. How much exactly had she heard of his conversation with his gram earlier?

He supposed it didn't matter. It wasn't like he was hiding anything. Not on purpose. But sometimes there just wasn't much point in taking all the crap out of your heart and examining it.

Without thinking any more about it, he took Riley's hand as they walked out of the room and down the hall, waving at the nurses, before getting on the elevator. At that point, there truly was no reason for him to still be holding it. Maybe she'd think he'd forgotten, when in reality, his whole focus was on the slim hand in his.

He shouldn't want to hold it, and as they stepped on the elevator— the last possible time anyone could see them, and with that, his last possible excuse for still cradling it in his—he made himself drop it. Like letting go of a lifeline.

The elevator doors closed behind them. Riley let out a deep breath. "I thought that went well."

"Yeah." He forced his mouth open. Maybe she still looked down on him. If she did, it hadn't interfered with helping him convince his gram they were married. "Thanks. I know I didn't give you an easy choice. Actually, I kind of pushed you into this, but I appreciate the fact that you took it seriously. That look on my gram's face made everything worth it for me. Thank you."

He'd been staring at the elevator door as he spoke, but he looked down to see her staring up at him.

"I didn't expect you to thank me," she said softly, her eyes a little wide and her brows slightly lifted.

He wished she'd quit looking at him like that. It made him want to do more than hold her hand. He looked back at the elevator door. "Why wouldn't I?"

She shrugged. "We made a deal. I'm just keeping my end."

"It's not a given, in today's world, that you would do what you said you were going to do." They had never made any promises to each other, so that wasn't a slam. It was a simple statement of fact.

She nodded. She'd worked with the same kinds of people he had. She knew it to be true.

The door opened. He pulled the parking ticket out of his pocket and walked to the machine to pay.

Focusing on what he was doing, he said, as casually as he could, "What did your dad want?"

"How'd you know it was my dad?"

"I saw it on your phone." Even if he hadn't, he would have guessed by the look on her face. The one that was half fearful, half determined. He got the feeling she'd do anything to make her dad happy or proud. A clawing and tightening ripped up his throat. Jealous? Of her dad? He almost snorted.

She straightened. "He was just confirming that he'd had our house here cleaned and staffed and ready for me...us...to arrive."

His hand stilled. The machine chirped at him to do the next step, but he just stared at the screen before slowly turning to her. "House?"

"Well, yeah. We have a house here, several actually, that we keep for when business associates visit or for family when they come in. The one that I always use when I come in happens to be about halfway between here and the terminal, and I just thought..."

"You thought wrong." His words were much harsher than he'd meant them to be. But the anger that moved like lava through his chest wouldn't let him say them any differently.

She blinked. Her eyebrows slowly raised. They stared at each other for several heartbeats. Him angry. Her defiant.

She stuck her chin out. "Where were you going to have us stay?"

He hadn't gotten that far, to be honest. Hadn't even thought about it. "A hotel, until I found a rental place. I can provide for myself and my wife."

She rolled her eyes. "Stop being a caveman."

His brows shot up, even though he had figured out on the way down that she would never appreciate the things he could offer her in exchange for what she'd already given him. "If providing for my wife makes me a caveman, I'll own it."

He turned back to the machine, punching in the buttons and swiping his card, letting her know he was done discussing it.

"Fine. You can stay wherever you want to. If you won't drop me off at my house, I'll get a cab."

She moved to walk away. His pride would never allow him to stop her. It wouldn't even let him watch.

"I'll drop you off," he said to the machine.

"Fine." That one word hit his back like a bullet.

Chapter Twelve

Riley walked with purposeful stride to Ben's pickup. The man was infuriating. They could stay in a house that was furnished, set up like a real married couple. Or they could be in a cramped hotel for a few days or so...however long it took him to find them a "rental" which, in her mind, did not bode well for comfort and furnishings.

It was a no-brainer.

It's a good thing she hadn't bet that Ben had a brain.

That wasn't nice. Seeing how gentle he was with his gram, how he cared for her, how he took Riley's hand in his and made her feel safe and protected and cared for. She could get used to walking by that man's side.

Then he had to go and be a Neanderthal.

She stopped at the passenger door and blew a breath out, waiting for the door to unlock, staring at her reflection in the window. She looked annoyed. Jacked off. And why?

Because the man wanted to take care of her.

Some of the anger stiffening her spine drained out. Isn't that what she was enjoying there in the hospital? Him holding her hand and that feeling of protection? Why would she get angry when he was just doing what she admired—taking care of her. Albeit, not in the way she wanted.

The lights flashed, and the locks clicked. She reached for the handle, but Ben's thick forearm cut in beside her, and he opened her door.

"Thank you," she mumbled.

She wasn't going to give in. Sure, she just realized she could see his side of things—he wanted to take care of her himself—but that didn't make him right. She wanted a furnished house and a comfortable bed.

He got in on his side and started the truck.

She'd just explained in as short a way as possible where her house was when his phone rang.

He answered on the hands-free.

"Twins," he said, and Riley's mouth tugged up.

"Yep, it's both of us." Eve's voice was a little more of an alto, and she spoke first. "How'd your wedding go?"

"Got hitched."

Eve snorted. "I guess it's a bit of a relief that you didn't all the sudden turn into a hopeless romantic, but still...poor Riley. Is she there?"

"I'm in the pickup." He looked over and met her eyes. "She's beside me."

Was there a deeper meaning in those words? It almost felt like there was. She was beside him. What was his brain trying to say?

"Hi, Riley!" the twins called.

"Hey, Eve. Eden."

"Has our big brother been treating you okay?"

"He's been great." Which was true.

"Are you guys booking the honeymoon suite at the local hotel?"

"I think we're staying at different locations tonight," she said. And for who knew how long. Riley glanced over at Ben and wished she wouldn't have said anything. His mouth had twisted. Yeah, he probably didn't want anyone, even the twins, knowing about their private life. She should have kept her big mouth shut.

"What?" Eden said. "You're not staying together? How are people going to believe you're really together if you're not...together?"

Ben's hands tightened on the wheel as he motored slowly out of the parking lot. Riley sighed and looked away.

"Why are you staying in different places? What different places?" Eve asked.

Ben didn't offer any explanation, and since Riley was the one who opened the can of worms, she figured she was the one who needed to eat it. She crossed her arms over her chest. "My family has a house. It's furnished and staffed, and it's ready for us. But your brother," she couldn't quite bring herself to say his name, "thinks we should stay in a hotel anyway and then look for a rental."

"Oh." Eve sounded disappointed. "So, you're not even married for a day, and you're having your first fight."

"We're not fighting," Ben said in a tone that sounded an awful lot like one he would use in an argument.

"Of course you're not." Riley could almost hear Eve's eyes roll through the truck speaker. "You just probably gave her some spiel about how you're the man so you have to provide everything, and she probably responded in a perfectly reasonable way that she'd rather be comfortable than cater to your pride."

It was too close to the truth, and neither of them said anything.

"And what she doesn't understand is that pride and providing is all you have, and what you don't understand is that a man's pride doesn't mean anything to a woman." Eden's voice ended on a soft note, almost like a plea for one of them to be sensible.

Ben kept driving.

"That sounds reasonable, Eden," Riley said. But there was no solution there.

"Very reasonable, Twin," Ben said, sounding unreasonable. "And so we made the also very reasonable decision to stay in different places tonight."

"Ben…" Eve drew his name out. "If this were Eden and I fighting, you know what you'd say."

"Someone has to give in," Eden supplied the answer.

"And that's the more mature person," Eve finished for her.

Ben's chest went in and out. His eyes never left the road. "Did you two actually want something? Or did you just call to harass us?"

"We missed you. The house makes all kinds of noises that we didn't notice before." She lowered her voice. "I think it might be haunted."

Ben shook his head and opened his mouth, but Eve started talking before he could. "We know, though, if there were any danger at all, you wouldn't have left. We've said that to each other a couple of times, and then we just wanted to talk to you. Because we can."

Riley looked out the window, staring into the darkness. Ben was a protector. And a provider. Eve and Eden both knew it. That's why they'd called him when they were scared of the house noises. And that's all he was trying to do with her. Protect. Provide.

Even though it made a lot more sense for them to just use the house, wouldn't it be big of her to let it go and allow Ben to do what he was good at?

As soon as the twins hung up, she would tell Ben she'd go to the hotel tonight and move into a rental place when he found one. Let him live his strength.

They chatted a bit more, with the twins saying they'd be down tomorrow evening and Ben promising to meet them at the hospital. They talked a little about their day and everything they needed to do in order to leave and come down. Riley listened. This was a side of Ben she'd really not seen. He was their brother, but he played the role of both mom and dad to them, and they obviously adored and respected him.

She had always thought of him first as a man she was attracted to and second as a great employee and a huge asset to their company. This side—the softer, gentler side—of Ben was intriguing and attractive.

He ended the call when they were just a few minutes from the turn for her house. She was lost in thought and didn't speak right away.

Beside her, Ben tapped the steering wheel. "You know, the girls were right. It's just my pride. Let's stay at your house. I'm sorry I made a big deal about it."

Her head whipped around. "No. You don't get to be the big person. I was going to say we'd just stay at a hotel like you said."

His eyes cut to hers, like he was judging whether or not she was joking. One side of his mouth kicked up, and he grunted. "Are we going to fight about it again, only on different sides?"

She laughed. A tension-easing laugh. "No. Let's stay at my house. It has six bedrooms. I'll have the staff get two more ready for Eve and Eden, and they can stay with us while they're here. It sounded like they're coming down for a while anyway?"

He shrugged. "We'll see how things go."

She could accept that answer. "I was hoping to go to the terminal tomorrow. Dad said next week, but we could get started early."

"If the guy I'm replacing is there, it could be awkward."

"It was a woman, and she's gone."

Ben made the turn down the road that led to her property. It was a dark lane, but the old fixed-up farmhouse glowed as they topped the rise.

Ben stared at it. "When you said 'staff,' what, exactly, did you mean?"

"Just a maid and a handyman. Nothing crazy."

"You have a maid and a handyman here?"

"They might not be in the house. There's a smaller house over there." She pointed off to the left where a smaller, darker home stood. "That's where they stay."

"They don't have families?" Ben still hadn't moved more than the few muscles it took to keep the slowly moving pickup on the drive.

"Well, my dad lives on the other side of town, about forty-five minutes away. That's where they usually work and where their families live. If I stay for any length of time, we'll hire my own staff, and Dad will get his back." It sounded rich as she said it, and she could only imagine how it came off to Ben. "Just think of it as one of the perks of being married to me. You're going to work your butt off for the company, and this is what you get in return."

"I get a paycheck in return." He stopped the pickup in front of the garage. "Not servants."

"Okay. So it's what you get for putting up with me."

His eyes slanted over. "Putting up with you hasn't been as hard as I was afraid it might be." He shifted into park and shut the pickup off. "You do snore, though."

"I do not!"

"It was kind of adorable, actually." He opened the door and hopped out.

She snored? She supposed that wasn't such a huge surprise, but no one had ever called her adorable before.

BEN OPENED RILEY'S DOOR. She looked surprised again, and he hid a smile. He liked surprising her.

Even if she did make him feel like he wasn't good enough because all he could provide was a cramped hotel room, not a house. With servants.

After his initial gut reaction that she was showing him how much better she was than him by insisting they stay in a house, he'd realized that she probably just wanted to be comfortable. The house wouldn't cost them anything and would be far nicer than a hotel. She hadn't been lording it over him. He needed to give her the benefit of the doubt.

He walked to the back and grabbed his duffel out of the pickup along with Riley's suitcase and three of her smaller bags. He'd carry the rest of the luggage in in a bit.

She'd walked to the door. "I'll have to have a copy of this key made for you."

"There's probably a machine at the shop that will do it." There'd been one in Maine, and that was a smaller place, so he'd assume that this terminal would have all that and more.

"Remind me to give it to you in the morning."

"I will. I'll have a copy of my pickup key made as well so you can drive it if you need it." He supposed that's what a real married couple would do. The line between when they faked it and when it was real was getting harder and harder to see, and they hadn't even been "married" that long.

It was funny, but when he allowed himself, he forgot what Riley had done and just enjoyed the woman she had become. She was still way out of his league. He needed to keep that in mind, or he was going to end up hurt over this.

The lock clicked, and she pushed the door open. He stepped into the roomy entry, hardwood floors polished and gleaming. A staircase had an old-fashioned wooden banister lining the length of it. Glistening lights hung from the ceiling, and everything looked picture perfect. A far cry from his comfortably worn home and furnishings. Cozy, comfy, and easy to clean were his main requirements in home décor. Here he felt like he'd stepped into a magazine.

The general unease that had been simmering in his chest since she'd mentioned having a house and wanting to stay there caught fire. He tried to snuff it out but was afraid that he only fanned the flames.

"I'll carry your stuff to your room if you tell me where it is." His voice sounded almost normal. Weird.

"You don't have to."

"Am I sleeping in the servants' quarters?"

"They're not 'servants' quarters.'" She put a hand on her hip. "And no, why?"

"Then I assume I'm going up, anyway. I've got your stuff. I'll carry it. Tell me where." Like he had to have a reason for offering to carry her stuff up.

"Okay. Follow me. I'll show you around." She led the way upstairs, and he followed, admiring the beautifully refinished woodwork and wide hall. "This room is mine." She opened the first door on the right.

He took a quick peek as he set her things down. Neutral colors. Sheer curtains in the windows. Nothing stood out to him. A generic room. A far cry from the bright colors, posters, and scattered clothes and books that made up his sisters' rooms.

"And here's the only other room with a master bath." She opened the door across the hall. A big, dark wood bed sat in the center of the room with dark wood dressers on either side. Definitely a masculine room.

"So, you guys did that on purpose—there's a girls' room and a boys' room?"

She chuckled as he set his duffel down. "Yep. That way we're ready for whoever needs it."

"I see." He was just one of many. Like a hotel, only he wasn't paying.

"Come on back downstairs. There should be some cold cuts and cheese for sandwiches. And I'll show you where everything is. Judy will make supper for us, but breakfast and packing a lunch are our responsibilities."

"Okay."

He and the twins had taken turns doing the cooking.

He followed her back downstairs, wondering why she had started wringing her hands together. Was he making her nervous? Or did she need to shake him so she could...make a call or something else?

They walked into the big farm kitchen. "There are always drinks in this fridge." She pointed to a big stainless steel appliance. "You're welcome to use the stove. There should be supplies in here, and if you don't have what you need or want, leave a note on the counter for Judy, and she'll see that we have it." Riley went on, pointing out the coffeepot, the microwave, and what was in each drawer. She hadn't chattered this much all day.

Her face was tight, and her movements jerky.

"What's up?" He cut into her monologue.

She stopped talking abruptly but didn't turn from where she stood in front of the dishwasher. She'd actually opened it and was telling him how to run it. Like he couldn't find the start button on his own.

"What do you mean?" she asked, her head still down.

He walked to the other side of the island and leaned his forearms on it. It didn't surprise him when she moved back until her hip hit the counter.

"That's what I mean." Had she suddenly decided he was a serial killer?

She swallowed; her hands gripped the counter behind her.

"Is it me making you nervous?" He straightened, leaning a hip against the island and crossing his arms over his chest.

She jutted her chin out. "It did occur to me that we are alone and this is a remote area—"

"Okay," he interrupted her again and pushed off from the counter. "I'll be back to pick you up in the morning. What time?"

He paused at the kitchen doorway and looked back when she didn't answer.

He'd never seen her look miserable before. Both lips were caught between her teeth. The confident businesswoman who he saw almost every day at the shop had totally disappeared.

Putting a hand on the doorway, he waited. Finally, she looked up, her eyes narrowed. She moved slowly around the counter and stopped in front of him. He didn't move. Half annoyed, half caught up in her scent and the attraction that had leapt to life between them.

He wasn't going to touch her. She'd as much as said she thought he'd jump her since they were alone together. Like he really was a caveman with no restraint. Maybe he should have made a snide comment about why anyone would want to, but he couldn't insult her like that. She might look strong, but words like that hurt. Not to mention, they weren't true. He didn't know what, exactly, he felt for her, but he couldn't hurt her. Not with his words, not with his actions, not with his hands. He gripped the polished doorframe.

She had stopped right in front of him. The silence in the kitchen screamed in protest. His heart thumped. Her confident, feminine scent drifted like soft butterflies around his nose. He breathed it in, and it hit his lungs, sweet and full. His eyes lowered, searching her face, reading the red on her cheeks, the pink of her tongue as it touched her bottom lip, the sweep of her lashes, and the arch of her neck.

She didn't touch him but was so close their breaths mingled when she looked up. He didn't move.

Lines appeared on her forehead. "I'm sorry. Please don't go."

He opened his mouth. She placed a hand on his chest. To stop him? To keep him quiet? Whatever the intention, it had the effect like water on a hot skillet. It surprised him that there was no sizzle and no steam. His chest burned. He clenched his jaw shut.

"I trust you. What I just said was stupid. It bothers me that I actually trust you more than any person I know. Anyone. And we're not even really on the same side. I mean, yes, I'm helping you and you're helping me, but it's not like we even really like each other that much. It made me nervous. Why do I trust you?" She looked down. "And everyone I've ever trusted before has let me down."

It was ironic that the only woman he'd ever allowed close to him was the one who had stabbed him in the heart and was now the one who stood in front of him, telling him she trusted him more than anyone else in the world. The irony almost overrode the electricity that snapped between them. Almost.

"I know how that feels," he said, his voice more gravelly and rough than an old motor on a cold morning.

Recognition flashed across her face. He almost felt bad for the jab, but he needed the distance it provided. Although he couldn't move out from under her hand; he wanted to cover it with his own and press it closer to his heart.

"I'm sorry for that, too."

"It was a long time ago, and it doesn't matter anymore."

"It was the worst mistake of my life."

It had been the hardest trial of his. He'd lost his mother. He'd run away from his father. He'd accepted the responsibility for his sisters and lied to be able to work full-time to support them while still going to school. He'd done it all and gone through everything, but nothing had hurt like the betrayal of the woman in front of him.

He wasn't about to tell her that.

Instead he lifted her hand, wrapping his own around it, feeling the rubber O-ring that had taken the place of a real ring. Whatever he'd been going to say or do flew from his mind when he touched her finger.

"I think we need to go buy you a ring before we do anything else tomorrow."

"I have a ring from my grandmother that I brought with me. I didn't think about it before the wedding, but when I was packing, I found it..." Several beats of loaded silence fell between them. "I would have put it on, but I didn't want you to think..." She trailed off, yet again.

"Think what?" he prompted.

"Think, first of all, that the ring you gave me wasn't good enough. And secondly, I didn't want you to get upset and think that I...that I was trying to make this," she motioned between them, "us, real."

"Wear your grandmother's ring. I appreciate the consideration for my feelings. The line between fake and real seems to blur and shift. It's hard to decipher where it's actually at sometimes." As he spoke, their hands seemed to move with minds of their own, and they shifted. Their fingers threaded together. Heat traveled up his arm to his elbow. He was playing with fire, no doubt.

If he were one of his sisters, he'd tell her to get a hotel room and spend the night reinforcing her heart with concrete.

Instead, here he stood, staring into Riley's eyes and allowing her to take another chunk out of the barrier protecting his scarred and broken heart.

He dropped his hand from the doorframe and at the same time pulled his fingers away from hers. "It's been a long day. That's a heck of a drive, and I didn't snore the afternoon away."

"I can't believe you're accusing me of snoring."

"I knew I should have videotaped it."

Her mouth opened and closed. "You'd better not have!"

He grinned then headed toward the stairs. "I didn't."

"Aren't you hungry?"

There had hardly ever been a time in his life where he couldn't eat. But he needed distance. He needed to remind himself that he didn't like Riley and that she'd choose her dad and his company over him again if she had the chance. Obviously, she was still his greatest weakness. Today had shown him that if nothing else. He needed to refocus and regroup.

"I'm more tired than anything else." He put a hand on the banister and started up the stairs. "It's a beautiful house. Thanks for letting me stay. I'll see you in the morning."

"Good night." Was there a wishful tone in her voice, or maybe it was his imagination? He wasn't sure. He couldn't let it matter.

Chapter Thirteen

Dawn was breaking when Riley went out for her run. She'd measured the distance and had run the same path many times over the years when she'd stayed at the old farmhouse. Somehow today it seemed different.

She could blame it on the ring she wore or the fact that today was the first day of her new position and trying to get this terminal not only in the black but to the top of the company. But it wasn't any of that.

It was the look in Ben's eyes last night as he'd held her hand and she'd admitted that what she'd done to him had been her biggest mistake. When she'd rejected him, brutally and publicly, she knew it hurt him. It had killed her, and she wasn't even on the receiving end.

Last night, from the look in his eyes before he'd shifted and it had disappeared, she'd realized that the pain was still there.

As she jogged back up the lane, the object of her thoughts stood outside in a t-shirt, leaning against the side of his pickup, his arms crossed over his chest and his muscles bulging, talking to Jason, the caretaker. Something Ben said made Jason throw his head back and laugh. They were probably about the same age. Jason was a little less husky, slightly taller. Ben looked more rugged, especially dressed for work in his black t-shirt and dark jeans and work boots. Jason wore the uniform of the caretakers—a green polo and dark khaki pants.

They laughed again. This time, Ben's gaze sharpened as he saw her jogging up the drive. His whole body seemed to stiffen, and his eyes lasered on her. Self-consciousness wasn't something she was normally plagued with, but she suddenly had the urge to check to see if her long-sleeved tee and tights were on correctly. Her hair bounced around in a ponytail, and she wore no makeup. Sweat dripped down her temple, and her face was probably beet red from the exertion and cold.

Tempted to jog right by, she stopped, panting with her hands on her knees. She wasn't trying to look good for him. She shouldn't care what he thought. Even if she hadn't been able to get him off her mind.

"Hey, Riley," Jason said pleasantly. He'd been a dependable worker for several years now. His family owned a lawn care service, and he worked on that on the side. A good, conscientious worker.

"Jason," she said. She almost had her breathing under control. "How have you been?"

"Just fine. I was telling Ben that Judy thought she saw a mouse yesterday in the hall, and I thought she was going to climb out that little window at the top of the stairs."

Riley shivered. "A mouse?"

"Turned out it was a dust ball that a draft had skittered along the floor. She squealed like the entire Second Brigade was after her."

"I think I might have too."

"You'd probably look just as funny as she did trying to climb the wall to get away from it."

"I don't think I'd climb the wall. Just run down the steps, maybe, then get a blowtorch or something and burn the house down to get rid of it." Riley wiped the sweat off her forehead and shook her legs out.

"Wow." Ben's lips curved up. "Do you think you'll wake me up first? Or should I invest in a box of smoke detectors?"

She looked up, meeting his smiling eyes. A warmth that had nothing to do with her run settled in her chest. "I'll wake you up unless the mouse runs into your room. That happens, you're on your own."

He lifted a brow. "Thanks."

Shaking the feeling of comfortable familiarity that had wrapped around her heart, she started for the house.

"I started coffee. Wasn't sure whether you drank it or not..."

"You mean you guys are married and you don't know whether she drinks coffee in the morning?" Jason asked incredulously.

Riley jerked to a stop.

Ben froze.

Then Jason got a smirky grin on his face. "Ha ha. I guess you guys have been too busy in the morning doing other things to worry about drinking coffee. Guess I have a lot to look forward to."

He smacked Ben with a resounding thwack and headed back across the yard. "I can tell when I'm not wanted. I'll tell Judy to hang out over here with me for a while." His laugh carried back across the grass.

Riley met Ben's stare. "Sorry," he said softly.

She shook her head. "Not your fault. Us not knowing each other could make things awkward at times."

He stepped up beside her, and they walked into the house together. "You know, I never asked what your dad said when you told him we were married."

Riley paused, her foot on the top porch step. "I didn't tell him."

"What?" Ben's voice was sharp.

Riley tried to dismiss it, although it wasn't something that could be brushed off, and she knew it. "I didn't tell him." She shrugged.

If Ben's eyes could shoot poison-laced arrows, she'd be dead. He finally moved to open the door for her. "When, exactly, were you going to tell him?"

"I guess I'll do it today."

"You guess? So, like, you were going to keep this from him?"

"No." That wasn't a bad idea actually. "Unless you think we can."

The door slammed shut much harder than necessary. Riley knew she was being unreasonable, but telling her dad that she'd gotten married the way she had wouldn't have been easy in any circumstances. Telling him she had married a mechanic...that she'd married Ben...

"You're afraid." Ben stated the obvious in a tone of voice that left no confusion as to how he felt. But she didn't really understand why he was so upset. After all, it wasn't like they were going to stay married. If she could keep it from her dad for six months, she and Ben would go their separate ways, and her dad would be none the wiser. It wasn't like her dad cared about anything but his business anyway.

The thought of Ben leaving ruined her good mood. She went to the counter and poured a coffee, setting it on the table. Then she went to the sink and filled a glass of water. She took a couple big gulps of the water.

Ben crossed his arms and leaned against the counter.

"Yeah. It's not going to go over well." She looked him in the eye. "Dad doesn't always pay that much attention to me, and even though he'll be at the same complex, my office is in a different building. I might only see him once or twice a week, and even then, we'll only discuss business. I can see him not even noticing that we're married for the six months that we agreed on." It was all business all the time for him. He'd come to her high school graduation, but mainly because he'd been the speaker. He'd missed her college graduation. She honestly wasn't sure he knew he missed it.

"You're saying you don't want to tell him?" Ben hadn't moved.

She nodded. "I definitely don't want to tell him. I'm saying I think I could get away with not. And if he notices," she shrugged, "I can cross that bridge then."

"So, we'll play the married thing down while we're at work, and we'll play it up while we're with my family?" There was a hard edge to his voice that had never been there before. She ignored it.

"That would be great. But—" She held up a finger. "I know that our agreement was we'd get married, I'd be your wife, you'd come to Pennsylvania and help me here at Coleman. If it comes down to a choice, I will never pretend to not be married. I'd just like to see if I can get away without telling Dad."

He rolled that around in his head. Convoluted logic, she knew. But it could work.

She could tell he didn't like the idea by the twist of his lips and the way he turned his head away. A muscle in his jaw popped in and out.

Riley watched, fascinated. He was angry. It wasn't his anger that fascinated her, though. It was the fact that she wasn't afraid of it. Not like she was of her dad's anger. Her dad wouldn't hurt her, but when he was angry, it was hard to tell what exactly he'd do. Ben's controlled anger was actually soothing. A refreshing change.

"I never even thought I should have gotten his permission." He ran a hand through his short hair. "Crap. It never even crossed my mind."

Riley just stared at him. That's what he was worried about? "That's really old-fashioned."

He looked up from under his brows. "I'd expect it of anyone who wanted one of my sisters."

She appreciated his consideration. "This wasn't exactly a regular marriage."

"I know. But he doesn't know."

"Trust me. He's not going to care about that."

"It's not even a matter of him caring. It's a matter of my principles and how easily I ignored them to get what I wanted." He threw his arms down in frustration and paced over to the window, bracing his hands on either side of the sink. "I guess that's what I get for lying in the first place."

"I'm afraid our lying isn't done."

"Yeah. It's just started."

AT SIX THAT EVENING, Ben put the last of his tools away and let the second shift supervisor know he was leaving. He texted Riley back that he'd meet her where she suggested—in front of the security shack—and then texted Eve and Eden that he'd be at the hospital at seven thirty to meet them.

Riley was waiting when he pulled up, and she hopped in before he could put the truck in park and open her door.

The tension that lined her face and the droop of her shoulders suggested her day hadn't gone any better than his. He refrained from asking, figuring she'd talk when she was ready. He liked a little time to decompress, not that he'd ever had it with the twins around.

It was nice to ride in silence. There was always a radio on in the shop. The type of music depended on the tastes of the shift foreman. Sometimes the shop foreman pulled rank.

It was all loud and clanging, and in Maine, he'd taken to wearing earplugs when he worked.

Riley sat beside him with her head leaned back on the seat, her eyes closed. He was tempted to tease her about starting to snore, but she looked so dejected, he decided not to bother.

Finally, about five minutes from the turn to her family's farmhouse, she opened her eyes and looked over. "Thanks for giving me a minute."

"That bad?"

"Worse." She picked her head up. It looked like she was getting her second wind. "You?"

He shrugged. "Nothing I can't handle."

"I can handle it too. I'm just dreading it." She gave a little smile.

"You have the added pressure of your dad."

"Yeah."

"All I have is the challenge, and I'm looking forward to it." It was the honest truth. There was a female mechanic that he figured was going to give him trouble. Either by messing with one of the guys or trying to mess with him. With the strict harassment policies, there couldn't be anything that remotely hinted of that. And unfortunately, it was almost always the man who was punished or fired. In this case, he was sure it was the woman who was going to be causing the problem. But Riley didn't need to be burdened with that.

Everything else would be easy.

He flipped the turn signal on. "I can't go in on the first day on the job and start making a bunch of changes. Everyone resents it."

"Yeah. I figured you knew that." She sighed. "My problems are less changes that need to be made in the workplace." She snorted. "At least for now. It's more that everyone who has come before has left the computer system in such a mess, I can't figure a thing out."

"Maybe you need someone from IT?"

"He didn't know anything, either."

"Isn't it the same system that you used in Maine?"

"It is. But nothing is organized. There are no spreadsheets. I can't find employment files. I did find some quarterlies from last year, but they weren't in with anything else that had to do with anything..." She let out a breath. "Let's just say, if we do this, it's going to be a miracle. At least on my end."

He slowed as they came to the house. "Don't worry about my end. It's good."

She tilted her head over. "Thanks so much. Even if you're lying through your teeth right now, your confidence is making me feel better."

Without thinking about it, he reached over and cupped her cheek. "I'm not lying. There's nothing in that shop that I can't handle. They've got every machine I would ever need." Even if he didn't know how to run several of them. "And I met a few good, solid guys today. One good guy who knows what he's doing is worth five who screw off all day. I know that I've got someone who has my back," he was talking about her, "so when I start to make those necessary but painful decisions, I'll be good. I've got guys on the floor who will work. I've got a woman upstairs in the office who will back me, and I know the system. I just have to adjust for three shifts instead of one."

Her cheek was soft under his hand. He ran his thumb over her skin. Her eyes filled. He searched her face. "What?" he asked softly.

She took a shaky breath. Then her hand came up to press against his. "Thanks," she breathed out, low and sincere. They stared into each other's eyes as the seconds ticked by. He didn't know how long they sat there, but he felt the pull, strong and hard. Riley was everything he'd ever thought and so much more. But he couldn't fall for his fake wife.

Riley cleared her throat, breaking the spell that had fallen around them. "Come on. We'll just have time to eat and shower before we have to head to the hospital. We've got the other side of the family's problems to deal with."

Chapter Fourteen

They met the twins on the highway exit. Eve drove Riley's car, and Eden drove the car they shared. They left both cars there and piled into the back seat of Ben's pickup.

"That guy looks exactly like you, Ben," Eve said as they pulled into the hospital parking lot.

Ben glanced over. A tall, broad-shouldered man with dark hair and eyes, wearing a black t-shirt and jeans, leaned against the building with his arms crossed over his chest and one booted foot braced against the wall behind him.

It had to be one of his half brothers. It wasn't quite like looking in the mirror but close. The dude wasn't smiling, either.

"That must be the welcoming committee. They missed us last night." Ben wanted to ease the looks of consternation on his sisters' faces. This was part of the reason he'd never tried to get in touch. If his half brothers were anything like his dad, they were mean, low-down snakes. Not people he wanted his sisters to have to deal with. Too late now.

"Should we send a delegation out to smoke a peace pipe before we all try to enter the sacred hunting grounds?" Eden asked with a dramatic shiver.

Ben eyed her in the rearview. "Why don't you just say, 'Ben, that dude looks scary. Go make sure he's not going to hurt us.'"

"Because I would sound like a two-year-old if I said that."

"Oh, versus sounding like a four-year-old by talking about peace pipes and hunting grounds?"

Riley and Eve chuckled. Eden rolled her eyes. "I was trying to ease the tension."

Ben grabbed the latch on his pickup. He looked across the seat at Riley. "You okay for a minute?"

She nodded. "I've got a can of mace, and I'm not afraid to use it."

"Not on me, hopefully."

"I'm afraid it would be easy to get you two mixed up." She nodded over at the man who hadn't moved but watched them with an intensity that stirred Ben's neck hairs.

"Yeah." He pushed his door open. "Maybe he's just out there on a smoke break."

"And maybe he's packing. Be careful, Ben. He doesn't look like someone I'd mess with."

"Don't worry, Riley." Eden reached up and patted Riley's shoulder. "Ben deals with guys like that all the time."

Ben got out and closed the door. He let his hands hang at his sides as he strode over. The guy straightened, watching him with the same brown eyes that stared back out at him from the bathroom mirror every morning. Ben stopped a few feet from him.

The guy didn't say anything, and Ben considered waiting, but he was the oldest. He probably needed to speak first. He took his best guess. "Torque?"

The guy's head jerked up. His eyes were honest and clear. Ben had worked with a lot of different kinds of men through the years, including some that were pretty shady. He'd also worked with a lot of decent, hardworking men. He'd become a fairly good judge between the two.

Torque was honest and upright. Ben's heart cracked.

He held out his hand. "It's good to see you, brother."

Torque's eyes moved from his face to his hand and back again. Then he straightened and grabbed Ben's hand. Ben jerked him forward into a big bear hug. Torque hugged him back.

They parted, but Ben kept his arm around Torque's wide shoulders. "Last time I saw you, you were about this tall and ugly as a mud fence." He held out his hand waist high. "You grew, anyway."

Torque's grin revealed straight, white teeth. "Better watch with the insults. You're my mirror image."

"Think you got that backwards, little brother."

Torque laughed. "Your wife and sisters getting out?"

Ben looked back at the pickup. Riley understood and got out immediately. Eve and Eden followed.

"Nice-looking family."

Ben's head swiveled around. It was on the tip of his tongue to tell Torque hands off, but then he realized that Torque meant it as a sincere compliment.

"Those are your sisters too."

"They must favor your mom. Especially the blond."

"That's Eden. And yeah, she looks just like Mom." He ran a hand through his hair. Did one ever recover from losing one's mother? "The other one's Eve. She has our dark hair, but Mom's delicate bone structure."

"Wow. Fancy words. Guess I mighta ended up like that if I'da had sisters."

"Women," Ben agreed. They shook their heads together.

Riley walked up and slipped her arm around his waist like they'd been married for years instead of one day. He could have kissed her.

"This is my wife, Riley."

She held out her hand, and Torque shook it carefully.

"It's great to finally meet you," she said.

"Same," Torque answered.

"Eve and Eden, this is your brother, Torque."

They both shook his hand, eyeing him up and down.

No one really seemed to know what to say. Ben was too busy trying to keep his focus anywhere but on the slim arm that encircled his waist.

Finally, Torque broke the awkward silence. "Come on. Gram's doing better today."

～

AFTER AN HOUR and a half in the hospital room where they'd met Tough and Turbo and their wives, Kelly and Harris, Riley was exhausted. Harris, the one redhead in the room, had the only chair, since someone had said she was pregnant. The way Turbo babied his wife gave Riley the idea that they viewed their pregnancy as a small miracle. Apparently, there were other kids, belonging to the other couples, but they'd not brought them to the hospital. The adults were enough. Several of them at a time waited in the waiting room anyway.

Ben seemed to have a good time getting to know his brothers. She'd gotten separated from him, and she stood between Harris and Cassidy, who were deep in a conversation about babies, bottles, breastfeeding, and nap schedules, even though she had no clue about any of that stuff.

When the nurse came in to check vitals, Cassidy walked over to talk to Torque. Riley felt a warm hand slide around her waist.

"You okay?" Ben's deep voice asked softly.

She was much better now. "I'm fine." His arm was strong and hard and felt perfect around her. She'd taken a chance earlier when she'd walked to him and put her arm around him. There was no softness in the man, and he'd felt hot and alive under her touch. Her arm had sparked, and she'd wanted to move into his heat.

Even now, all she could think about was his arm around her. It blocked the rational thoughts from her brain.

"You look exhausted," he said, like his arm wasn't driving her crazy.

She tried to do the impossible and ignore it. "I'm sorry. I'll try to smile more."

"I wasn't complaining, I was stating a fact." His eyes skimmed over her face again. "Never mind. I'm taking you home."

"But you've just met your brothers after twenty years apart, and your gram…"

He put a finger on her lips and bent his head. "I'm glad about my brothers, and I love my gram, but it's my job to take care of you. Let me do my job."

Was he saying that for the benefit of any of his family who might be listening? Riley glanced covertly around. None of them were paying attention. She lifted her face. Ben's was right there. His eyes, concerned, filled her vision. The stubble on his chin called to her. A slight tug on her waist and she moved a step closer. The rest of the world faded away, and everything was just Ben and her. His breath and hers. His heartbeat and hers. Until it all became one.

"I think Ben and Riley need to go home." Turbo, not quite as tall as the other brothers but with wider shoulders and the same dark hair and eyes, came over with the same grin he'd worn all evening. "Your woman looks exhausted."

Although her father owned a trucking company, Riley had spent more time with the office employees than the guys outside. Ben's family was a little rougher than the businessmen and millionaires she was used to socializing with. Even though the whole "your woman" felt very cavemanlike, she was sure, by the open, friendly look on Turbo's face, he didn't mean anything by it. Ben's family might be rougher, but they were also more real.

Still, Riley tried to pull back. She wanted to look like Ben's wife, not his "woman," but Ben's arm stayed around her like a steel band. She allowed her body to melt into his side. They faced Turbo together.

"I think Turbo has a great idea. We've had a big week. You girls ready to go?"

The twins came over and kissed their gram goodbye. "We'll be back tomorrow," Eve promised.

Ben let go of Riley and hugged each of his brothers. Riley couldn't help but smile at the look of happiness on Gram's face. If it were possible for joy to heal, Gram would be better in no time.

Finally, they were walking out of the hospital. The twins stopped to use the restroom, while Riley and Ben validated their parking ticket.

"Thanks," Ben said as they waited for the twins at the exit door. He held her hand. She didn't even think about trying to pull it away. She wanted him to hold it. In fact, if he'd put his arm around her, it would be even better.

As though he could read her mind, he pulled her back toward him until she leaned back against him. He tucked her head under his chin and wrapped both of his arms around her waist, never letting go of her hand.

In the back of her head, warning bells were going off. But he felt so solid and strong behind her. After the crazy day she'd had, she didn't want to face reality.

She relaxed back into him. His chin rested on her head. His warmth seeped through her.

"We made it through day one, I guess," she said.

His arms squeezed then released a little. "I thought I'd have to remind myself that I was supposed to pretend to be your husband. I'm finding it's harder to remember that I'm really not."

Riley's heart stopped. His words sent shivers out her fingers and down through her toes.

"Never know when someone in my family might come out behind us."

Her heart froze. He'd just been holding her because of his family? Disappointment bit hard, and it stung.

Before she could answer, the twins came out. "You two ready?" Eve asked with a look askance at their cozy position.

"We are." Ben dropped his arms. He didn't grab her hand again as they all walked together to the pickup.

FRIDAY MORNING, Ben was up and out on the front porch before dawn. If one could get up when one never really slept. It had been amazing to be reunited with his brothers. Part of him hated the fact that he'd let fear keep him from reaching out long before this. He'd missed twenty years with three men he was proud to call family. Who'd have looked at his dad and thought that a man like that could have sons like Torque, Tough, and Turbo?

Gram deserved a lot of that credit, he knew. Since he had only been concerned about protecting his sisters. He'd done what he thought was best at the time. He'd been so focused on surviving, on paying the bills and raising his sisters after his mother died that he hoped he could really be excused for not being able to have more than that in his life.

So, sure, part of the reason he couldn't sleep was the fact that his old life had intersected with his new, and his whole family, at least all his siblings, was together at last.

But that really wasn't what kept him up all night.

Riley.

She had felt so good in his arms. Like she belonged there. Like the past never happened. Like she'd never paraded past him with another boy on her arm and hadn't said he was a poor boy who wouldn't amount to anything and she wasn't interested.

Was she leading him on now? Was she just playing her part when her hand slid into his and her body melted against him? Were the looks she gave him under her lashes, the ones that said she admired him and was grateful, were those fake too?

God knew he had enough trouble keeping his acting and his real emotions separate. Heck, there wasn't any acting on his part. Everything he'd felt for her back when he was young and dumb as dirt was all right there in his heart now. And he was stuck with her for another six months. There was no way he was walking away from her without ripping a part of himself out. It was going to hurt, no doubt. He wasn't sure, though, that he had what it took to put more distance between them. Everything in his heart and soul longed to be closer.

He'd better enjoy this time with his family because he was going to have to move to Antarctica to get away from the attraction he felt toward his *wife* and the web of lies he'd spun for himself.

How could he protect his heart, when the whole reason for their deal was so his family would believe they were married? For real.

He stretched a hand up the banister pole and leaned against it. Sure, there were problems to solve in the shop, but they were nothing compared to the problem of his runaway feelings for Riley.

The door cracked open behind him. He didn't need to turn to know it was Riley. The twins didn't make the hair on the back of his neck stand at attention. They didn't smell that good, either.

"Hey, wife," he said without turning around.

"Hey, husband," she imitated, and he smiled. Man, he wished she didn't make him feel like the king of his castle.

"As exhausted as you looked yesterday, I thought you'd sleep like a rock."

"I did." She drifted over and sat down on the top step at his feet, wrapping her arms around her legs. "But I dreamed that my dad found out about us, and then all I saw was blood, and I knew it was yours." She shivered. "I didn't even try to go back to sleep."

What would she do if he did what he wanted, which was to walk over, sit down on the step behind her, a leg on either side of her, and cradle her between his knees? Would she lean back into him? His heart thundered. Could he wrap his arms around her and watch the sunrise with his wife in his arms? Arms that ached to hold her. He'd put his lips on her hair and breathe deeply of her scent, allowing it to fill his lungs and his body, taking a part of her with him as he faced his day. He closed his eyes against the desire that rose like manifold heat in his chest.

He shook the thoughts, but the painful longing in his body to be closer to her didn't ease.

He forced himself to speak. "Your dad might be ruthless in business, but he's not going to hurt me."

"He did once before."

Oh, she was wrong about that. It hadn't been her dad.

It had been her.

Ben didn't argue. She needed comfort, so that's what he gave. "He's not going to hurt you, either."

"I know." She pressed back, rocking while holding her legs close to her chest. "You know how dreams can be."

Did he ever. But she wasn't talking about the dreams he'd had of her. So, he answered with something other than what he was feeling. "Yeah. Eden used to have night terrors. She'd wake up screaming. I didn't know what the frig to do. That's scary. For her and me."

"For Eve, too, probably."

"No. Eve could sleep through a bomb blast."

"You know you'd make the best dad."

He didn't say anything. After Riley was finished shredding his heart, he'd kept his focus on raising his sisters. He had his mom's death to deal with too. For him and his sisters.

"You never got married."

"I did two days ago."

She harrumphed. "You know what I mean."

"Neither did you."

"I know. But it's hard to have any kind of life working the way I do.

Dad is pretty demanding. Not that he stands over my shoulder, but he wants results. Not to mention, after I got old enough, he's had me take Mom's place at a lot of charities and events."

"Yeah, I guess it was the same for me. The twins took up a lot of time, and I wasn't bringing a woman home who wasn't going to love them like I did."

"That was big of you. Surely you wished for help."

"Every day."

He willed his mouth to stay shut. He wasn't going to say that no woman compared to her. That he couldn't get the pieces of his broken heart back together. That if he couldn't have her, he didn't want anyone. That after the pain he endured with her, he would never trust anyone again anyway.

The sky in front of them turned gray, then pink, then orange.

He had six months of this. Six months to enjoy the presence of the only woman he'd ever loved. Then he was going to leave.

Chapter Fifteen

The next week, Riley sat at her desk in her new office, which was very similar to her old one, and leaned her forehead in her hands. The headache that had been knocking on her forehead all afternoon had exploded into a pounding pain just after five. At least it waited until everyone else went home.

She grabbed some pain pills out of her purse and chugged some of the water from the bottle on her desk.

She had never figured out whether there was any kind of rhyme or reason to the filing habits of her predecessor, and she'd stopped trying. The main focus now was getting all the files in order, from wherever they were. She'd gotten a good start on it last weekend when Ben had driven back to Maine to get his toolbox and make sure the house was closed up. It was funny how she'd missed him for the night he was gone.

She'd especially missed sitting on the porch with him watching the sunrise. They'd done that every morning since the first morning. The thought that it was going to be hard to watch him leave for good pushed up in her head, and she shoved it back. She didn't want to think about that. Didn't want to think how she loved feeling his quiet strength and sharing her problems.

With her dad, it was all about her performance. With Ben, she felt like a part of a team. An elite team, since Ben was so good at his job, and she was decent at hers. She felt like they could take the world by storm and end up sitting at the top. Although the goal wasn't to be at the top of the world. It was just to have this terminal at the top.

And with Ben, she knew she could do it. But the partnership with Ben, the feeling that they were so much stronger than the sum of their parts, was not long-term, and she needed to remember that.

She should focus on how pleased her dad was going to be when this shop was on the top of the performance list.

Like her thoughts had brought him up, her dad walked in her open office door.

Confident as always, he strode right in, not looking surprised that she was working late. Of course not. He'd expect it.

"I'm heading out on a trip for a few days," he said without a greeting. "I wanted to see what you're doing first. It's been a week. You're settling in?" He walked around her desk, looking at the information on her computer screen.

"It's going really good, Dad. I think in six months this terminal will be at the top."

Her dad crossed his arms over his chest and nodded silently, reading over her shoulder. She slid over a little to give him better access. She'd been organizing the maintenance logs. He reached down and clicked through a few places.

After a few minutes of silence, he pointed to truck #7564. "The top end on this truck was redone three times in six months. The last time was two weeks ago. That should throw a red flag up to people in the shop. Have you been in touch with anyone about that?"

"Well, it happened before we came, and I'm just now getting to these records..."

"How often have you been down in the shop since you got here?"

She strong-armed her smile to stay in place. "I'm there every day." When Ben dropped her off.

"Let's head down there for a few minutes now." Phrased as a suggestion, it really wasn't.

She closed a few windows and shut the computer off, dread making her head feel like the inside of a church bell on Sunday morning. How would she tell her dad she'd brought Ben along with her from Maine?

They walked out of her office together and headed to the shop. It wasn't a long walk, although the silence stretched between them like miles of empty desert, and the uncomfortableness of having nothing to talk to him about made each step seem like years passed.

Finally they reached the big garage bays where four of the eight doors were open, and she started chattering, listing off the things that had been fixed and the plans Ben had laid out for her.

Although she knew Ben wouldn't be on break, she really hoped he'd stepped out for something.

The open doors let in the cool evening air. A truck sat in each bay, one with the rears out, one with the motor torn down. Ben was redoing the motor, and he'd told her at lunch when she called him that he'd be working on getting everything apart until after nine. As she looked, he came around the side of the hood with a piston in his hand. His face broke into a grin as he saw her, then his eyes snapped to her dad. His smile froze.

She kept talking in her most business-like tone, hoping that Ben wouldn't force any issues or make a scene. Her dad might not even recognize him, but at the very least, she wouldn't have to admit today that she'd married him. That might go over a lot better once they'd gotten the shop performing to its potential.

But her dad stopped. His eyes narrowed on Ben as Ben set the piston on the makeshift worktable with the rest of the motor parts.

Riley altered direction, pointed away from Ben. "The shop layout is not conducive to performance. My team has some ideas that will improve production..."

Her dad stopped as Ben disappeared around the side of the truck. "That's the boy from Maine, isn't it?"

"That's Ben Baxter," Riley said in the same tone she'd been using. Her stomach flipped and flopped like a fish on land, but she kept her face placid. "And, yes, he was part of my team in Maine, and he agreed to come down here and help with this project."

"He's the one that had a thing for you back in high school."

Riley tilted her head and scrunched her face like she was trying to remember. "Really, Dad? High school? I'm focused on what I did yesterday and what I'm going to do tomorrow. I'm not thinking about silly high school crushes."

Her dad turned calculating eyes on her. "That's a big move to go from Maine to here. I'd watch him if I were you."

Riley laughed. It sounded fake to her ears, but her dad wouldn't notice. "Ben? He loves what he does, and he's good at it."

"Not what I'm talking about, girl. He'll manipulate you into giving him what he wants." His eyes narrowed. "You're worth a lot. To a boy like that, that can barely make a mortgage on a rundown bungalow on the shady side of town, you're a cash cow."

Even when she hadn't known Ben all that well, she wouldn't have thought for one second that he'd take something from her he hadn't earned. Her dad's words were intended to have the opposite effect, but she was more sure than ever that Ben didn't care about her money.

She knew better than to argue with her dad. "He's going back to Maine when we're done here." She turned and started off in a different direction.

Instead of following, her dad walked closer to the truck Ben was working on. Riley stopped and watched with the fascinated horror one might have as they watched a car accident about to happen.

"How many miles were on this motor, boy?"

Riley cringed. Her stomach bucked and jumped.

Ben's head appeared beside the turbo. "Almost a million."

"When were the rods and mains done?" her dad barked another question.

"At six hundred thousand," Ben answered easily.

"Is this a 550?"

"It's a 6NZ."

"How many of these have you done?"

"At least a hundred."

Riley almost smiled. There. That should ease her dad's mind.

But he wasn't finished. He leaned forward, and his voice lowered. "Stay away from my daughter. She's your boss, and you can remember your place, or I'll remind you of it with a nice, pretty pink slip."

Ben's eyes slipped to hers. She swallowed and looked away.

Ben's gaze never moved from her face as he answered, "Yes, sir." Of all the places in her life that she'd ever been, there was only one time and place that had been worse. Still, her mouth wouldn't open. Her brain kept saying, just six months. In six months, this will all be past.

Somehow that didn't help, because even though she knew Ben was leaving, he deserved so much more than the treatment she'd just given him.

Her dad moved away, and she followed. He stopped to talk to the other mechanic who was still working. He didn't know the answers to her dad's questions and had to stop working to go look them up. While her dad stood looking over his shoulder as the mechanic pulled the info up on the computer, Riley headed toward the parts room. It had been an unorganized mess when they'd come down last week, and she'd never remembered to ask Ben if he'd taken care of it.

The door was unlocked, and she stepped in and flipped the light on to find neatly stacked shelves and parts clearly marked with numbers and codes. A complete difference from just one week ago. Someone had spent a lot of time fixing this. She made a note to thank Ben. She'd bring her dad in here just as soon as he was done grilling the other mechanic on the history of the rears in that truck.

"So, you didn't tell him." Ben's voice came from the doorway.

She jerked her head around, her heart cramping painfully. He held onto the doorframe with one hand, his biceps bulging, his face an unreadable mask.

"No." Riley crossed her arms over her chest but didn't say any more because she had no excuses other than the ones she'd already given him.

"If you don't want to tell him, I can do it."

"He doesn't need to know. We can do this without him finding out."

His hand dropped from the doorframe, and he rubbed the back of his neck. "I know this is a fake marriage and everything, but am I really such a lowlife that you're too ashamed to admit to your dad that I'm nothing more than an employee that followed you down from Maine like some stupid puppy on a leash?"

She held her hands out, hating the shadow of pain that flickered across his face. Hating that she was hurting the proud, strong man who stood with her every morning as the sun came up. "I'm sorry. I don't want him to know. It'll just be easier."

"Easier doesn't equal better."

She put her hands on her hips. "We're married right now because it was easier for you to fake a relationship than to admit to your family you lied."

He looked away, a vein popping in his forehead, his fist clenched.

"Yeah," he finally said. "You're right. I guess though, when you're around my family, I don't treat you like some piece-of-trash stranger I barely know, lest anyone dare find out that we sit side by side on the porch of the house we share and watch the sunrise every morning."

The silence roared between them.

Her mouth opened, and words that she didn't want to say came out. "Fine. I shouldn't be out there with you anyway. It won't happen again." Her heart cracked, but her voice was strong. "You need to..."

Her dad's head appeared behind Ben's shoulder. Her eyes flickered to her dad then back to Ben. "Thank you for reminding me to show this improved layout to my dad. You can go back to work now."

Ben didn't need to look at her dad to know he was there, and he gave a curt nod. "Yes, ma'am," he said before turning and walking out.

Riley got the feeling her heart went with him.

BEN WALKED into his brother Tough's shop early Saturday morning. After having Riley act like he was barely anything more than a dirty stranger to her dad yesterday, he'd stayed at the Coleman garage until after midnight finishing the motor he'd been working on and trying not to think about why her words had hurt him so bad. He'd left the house this morning before daylight.

He wasn't being fair to Riley. It wasn't part of their deal to tell her dad. And if she could get away with not telling him, it would be so much better for her. In six months or so, when this all blew over, and he left, she'd still be here with her dad and their company. She'd have everything to deal with. Of course, her dad would probably be thrilled that she "broke up" with the lowly mechanic, but still, it would be a stigma for her for the rest of her life.

He could ask himself over and over why he was pushing, but he knew. When she'd rejected him, she'd basically chosen her dad over Ben. Having her dad find out that she was married to him now would be a little bit of sweet satisfaction that would ease the sting of the past rejection. But that was his own satisfaction. It wasn't fair to Riley.

Her treatment in the shop yesterday in front of her dad had hurt him. She'd acted like he didn't mean anything to her. Like he was simply an employee and nothing more. It smarted. Right in his chest in the place that felt such peace and contentment when he had his arms wrapped around her at the hospital when they visited his gram.

His brain understood perfectly why Riley acted the way she did in the shop yesterday. His heart, on the other hand, didn't understand a thing. It had always been stupid when it came to Riley.

Ben shook his head. He had family to think about.

The twins were thrilled to be developing relationships with the family they never knew they had. He could only support them making as many memories as possible with their gram.

He had some time to make up for with his half brothers. Torque, he suspected, was a lot like himself. Turbo, laughing and happy, was everyone's friend. Tough hadn't said much in the hospital, and other than his protective attitude over his bubbly and friendly wife, Ben hadn't been able to read him.

Showing up at his auto garage at 5:30 on a Saturday morning was a colossally stupid idea. Tough was probably still snuggled up to his wife in bed wherever he lived. He'd probably wonder why Ben wasn't in the same position. Not that he'd want to.

That was a lie, and he tried not to lie to himself. She'd acted the way she had either out of habit or because she was afraid of her dad, or maybe some of both. It didn't make it hurt less.

When Ben tried Tough's shop door, it opened, and the smell of strong coffee greeted him. Lights were on, and he could hear two men talking with raised voices.

He strode over to a high makeshift table where two old men sat across from each other, a checkerboard between them. They were so engrossed in their argument that they didn't notice him walk up. Tough was nowhere in sight.

"Little early for an argument, isn't it?"

The men stopped talking and looked at him. One had a full head of snow-white hair; the other's hair follicles had all migrated to his eyebrows.

"That's not Torque," the one with hair said.

"I didn't say it was," the other said in a combative tone.

"I'm Torque's brother, Ben." Ben held his hand out to the guy with hair. He stood slowly, like he needed time to get his joints working. His old, gnarled hand gripped Ben's with a strength that surprised him.

"I'm Al." He pumped Ben's hand a few times. "And that cantankerous old fellow is Mr. Sigel."

Mr. Sigel stood in the same slow manner and took Ben's proffered hand. "I assume that you're also Tough's brother?"

"Of course he is, you old coot. He said he was Torque's brother, so that means he's Tough's too."

"Not necessarily," Mr. Sigel said with a knowing nod. "Kids today do things different. I know a family that has five kids, and every one of them has a different set of parents."

Al shook his head. "Tell him you're Tough's brother too," he said to Ben. "Can't you see the eyes?"

"I'm Tough's brother too." Ben kept talking before the men found something else to argue about. "Where's Tough?"

"He's writing his column."

Ben shoved his hands in his pockets. Column? He didn't ask because he didn't want to admit he didn't know anything at all about his brother.

"He's in the office over there." Al threw his hand out toward a door that was closed but not shut tight.

"Maybe he doesn't want to be disturbed," Mr. Sigel said in a simple tone, like Al was not quite all there.

"Then he can say, 'I don't want to be disturbed,'" Al replied in the same tone.

"But if he has to say that, then he was already disturbed." Mr. Sigel used his black checker to jump two red checkers as he spoke.

"Hey, wait. You can't do that!" Al pointed at the checkerboard and started explaining why that move was illegal. He threatened to get the official checkers regulation manual out. Ben hadn't realized there was such a thing.

He backed away and turned toward the door. Neither man noticed, both of them trying to talk over the other with one of them claiming he had the regulation manual memorized.

It was no wonder Tough hid in his office writing a "column" if that's what he had to deal with out there.

Ben knocked on the door and pushed it open.

Tough sat behind a computer screen, typing away.

He really did have a column. Must be a mechanic advice column or something.

Tough looked up.

"Mind if I come in?" Ben asked.

Tough waved with his hand. Ben stepped in and closed the door. He didn't have anything in mind to talk about, but the arguing could drive him bonkers.

"I didn't get to talk to you much at the hospital, and I'm off today." He'd decided to take it off. He wasn't scheduled to work, but he would have anyway. After yesterday, Riley could save her dad's company on her own today. He'd start again on Monday.

"Figured I'd come over and see if I could give you a hand. I could change a tire or something." He grinned.

Tough returned his smile with a knowing one of his own, and Ben's heart warmed at sharing a mechanic joke with his brother. Their skills went much deeper. Anyone could change a tire.

"What kind of column do you have?" Ben asked.

Tough got a thoughtful look on his face before he answered seriously. "A relationship advice column."

Ben blinked. Either Tough had the best poker face he'd ever seen, or he was dead serious. He looked dead serious.

Tough indicated the chair across from him. "Sit."

Ben sat.

Turbo was the jokester. Ben had Tough pegged as a straight shooter, and his gut instinct was hardly ever wrong. He made the decision to go with it.

"On the internet?"

"I'm syndicated."

That was big-time. Hard to believe. Tough would be...rich. Ben glanced around the small, nondescript office. "So, you have the repair shop on the side?" He nodded out the door.

Tough shrugged. "The column makes a lot of money, and my wife finds ways to use it to help people. The shop supports us."

"You really do have a column." Ben grunted a laugh. His brother was a romantic advice columnist.

"Try me," Tough said, his own lips tilting up. "Warning ya, I'm gonna write your answer."

Ben narrowed his eyes. He'd heard of that. People who didn't talk much but who painted or played an instrument or, in Tough's case, wrote and could express themselves much better.

"Fair enough."

"Give me a problem," Tough demanded. "In a relationship."

Ben stared at Tough, tempted. Tempted to ask what he needed to do to...what? Make Riley fall in love with him? Make her choose him over her dad? Make their fake marriage real? He didn't want any of that. Did he?

He didn't know what he wanted, but he also wasn't sure what to do.

"Make something up," Tough suggested.

Yeah. Because Tough thought he was happily married just like Tough was.

"Okay. How about this..." How to phrase it? He rolled it over in his mind before saying, "Instead of getting married for love, a woman marries a man because the man can do something the woman needs done, and she can't do it herself. She wants to impress someone else."

Tough leaned back on his office chair, his arms crossed over his chest. "Keep going."

Right. Ben leaned his forearms on his legs and clasped his hands together. "So, the man agrees if the woman will do something *he* needs done and can't do himself. They enter their bargain, and both of them keep their ends of the deal."

Tough waited.

Ben stared at his hands. "But one of them decides they want more. What should they do?"

"More what?"

Ben studied his fingers like he'd never seen them before. Finally, he said softly, "More than a fake relationship." There. He'd admitted it. He didn't want a fake relationship with Riley, he wanted the real thing. That's why he was so upset that she wouldn't even acknowledge him in front of her dad. He wanted to be more than just a mechanic in her family's shop. He wanted to be her everything.

"This is hypothetical?"

"Yeah."

"You sure?"

"Yes," Ben said firmly. For some reason, he trusted Tough. But the feelings he had for Riley had burned him badly once. It wasn't easy to put them out there, even in a hypothetical situation.

Tough linked his hands together behind his head and thought for a while. Ben tried not to squirm. This was his little brother. He shouldn't feel like a schoolkid waiting for the principal to announce how many days of detention he had. But the same crampy feeling in his stomach combined with sweaty palms and the intense desire to run away was a good imitation.

Finally Tough started writing. It didn't take long. He didn't say anything, just clicked, and the printer started spitting out a paper. He pulled it off the printer and folded it.

"It makes me nervous when people read my advice in front of me. Don't read it until after you leave." Tough stood. "You still helping?"

Ben stood with him. "Said I would."

Tough handed him the paper, and Ben folded it again and put it in his back pocket.

"That's great, 'cause I have a car on the lift with a knocking in the motor, and it's not the normal stuff."

Ben stopped with his hand on the door. "Those guys stay here all day?"

"Yeah. You get used to them."

Ben grunted. "If you say so."

Chapter Sixteen

Riley shuffled down the stairs still wearing her pajama pants. She'd been up earlier, but as she suspected, Ben hadn't been on the porch this morning, so she'd gone back to bed. After leaving the office at nine last night, she'd gone home alone—the first time since they'd been "married."

Eve had informed her that Ben texted the twins and let them know he was going to be late—like midnight. Apparently, that was his standard operating procedure—texting his sisters when his schedule was interrupted.

After the way she'd treated him, she didn't blame him for not texting her. And for not answering the single text she'd sent him.

But she'd waited up for Ben to come home. She didn't really intend to, but she was too restless to sleep, so she tried to read in bed. It wasn't until she heard his pickup that she was able to relax. She listened to his deep voice as he spoke with Eden, who had waited up for him, then she listened to him move in the room across the hall and heard the water in the pipes as he showered.

She'd finally felt like she could relax. But she hadn't felt like she could face him.

Her words and her actions had hurt him, and they left a bitter taste in her mouth, but she didn't know what to do about it. She did know that she didn't like herself very much. But she wasn't entirely wrong. Their deal had said nothing about her telling her dad, and Ben wasn't planning on staying once his part was over. She was under no obligation to screw up her life any more than necessary, because she was going to be dealing with the fallout when he left. Alone.

Was there another way?

GRAM GOT to go home from the hospital that evening, and Riley volunteered to take her since Ben's brothers had spent more time than they had at the hospital that week. She texted Ben, letting him know she was heading into the hospital at three and waiting for the discharge.

She was surprised when he texted back.

I'll be there.

He didn't say any more. She left the house before he got home and figured he'd show up at some point. She didn't expect him to be waiting by the main entrance.

Her heart skipped several beats as her eyes landed on him. He'd either not been working or had gotten cleaned up, since his jeans were clean and there was no grease or dirt on his arms which were folded across his chest.

When she saw him, his eyes were already fixed on her. It was amazing how that look from him could make her feel like the only woman in the world. He looked at her like there was no one else he'd rather be watching. It sent warmth down the back of her neck, and her stride quickened automatically.

She was still more than five feet away from him when she blurted out, "I'm sorry."

His arms came down, and he straightened from leaning against the front pillar.

She stopped when she was directly in front of him and had to crane her neck to look into his eyes. "I really am sorry. As soon as we get your gram settled at home, I'll tell my dad." She hadn't realized those words were going to come out until they did, but after she said them, it felt like a dark shroud had lifted from her soul. Ben deserved to be with a woman who was proud to be beside him. She might not be his forever girl, but that didn't give her the right to give him less than he deserved.

He shook his head. "You don't need to. And I'm the one that needs to apologize. It was never part of our bargain for you to tell anyone that we were married. It was wrong of me to expect it."

They had never signed anything when they got married. She could trust Ben to do what was right. Apparently he felt the same about her. But to hear him say it here—that he wasn't going to let his feelings get in the way of what they'd verbally agreed on—meant so much. Especially when she knew her words and actions had really hurt him.

"Are we good?" he asked, his brows scrunched together, his hands in his pockets.

"Yes." She jerked her head down.

"I'll try to do better." He pulled a hand out of his pocket and offered it to her.

She took it, unwilling to get into an argument about whose fault it was that they were arguing to begin with.

As always, feeling her hand sliding across his callouses, being enfolded in his dry warmth, having that protection and comfort sent a thrill up her arm and straight to her heart. They turned together and stepped into the hospital.

BEN GAVE his gram her nine p.m. pills along with a glass of water. "You sure you don't want some pudding or applesauce to eat along with this? Kelly left plenty."

Kelly, Tough's wife, had been shopping while he was at Tough's garage today. She'd stocked the fridge with more food than a classroom full of junior high boys could possibly eat, let alone one frail old woman.

"No. I've had enough pudding to last me a year. I want steak."

Ben looked over the bed at Riley on the other side. He appreciated having her today. Not only had she convinced Gram she was doing her a favor by letting Ben wheel her out of the hospital, but she'd been able to get Gram to take it easy in bed rather than clean her already spotless trailer.

He supposed it was his turn to try to deal with an unreasonable request. Steak? Seriously?

"Maybe tomorrow." That answer had always worked with the twins. Riley's mouth twitched.

His gram's lips turned down. "I'm not three. I'm a grown woman who's more than capable of deciding for herself what she wants to eat, and I want steak."

Riley took his gram's hand. "I'm sorry, Gram. But Kelly didn't bring steak. I actually checked the fridge because I was going to cook myself a big juicy rib eye." She gave Gram a conspiratorial look. "Something about being in the hospital makes me crave bloody meat."

"It's those skinny nurses." Gram wrinkled her nose, but she took the pudding Riley offered and shoveled a bite into her mouth.

Man, how much easier it would have been to raise the twins if he'd had Riley tag-teaming him. He'd missed a wife to handle the girl problems; he'd done the best he could. It would have been easier—Riley winked at him as Gram handed back the empty pudding container— and more fun, too.

He shoved those thoughts aside. That's what had gotten him into trouble yesterday. Mistaking the "fake" marriage for a real relationship. In a fake marriage, Riley got to choose whether or not her dad knew about them. In a real relationship, he had the right to insist she tell.

He handed Gram her book. "I'll be in in a bit to check on you."

"I want bacon for breakfast," Gram said as she turned the book toward her and opened to her bookmark.

"I'll keep that in mind," Ben said with another exasperated glance at Riley.

She grinned and walked out ahead of him.

They headed back down the trailer hallway, past the bathroom. "If I remember right, there's two bedrooms here." He opened the first door and switched the light on.

A shelf full of toys sat directly inside. There were a ton of stuffed animals on the bed but no sheets and blankets.

"I bet Cassidy took the blankets to wash them and didn't bring them back," Riley said. "Kelly told me one of her twins threw up the last time she stayed."

"With Gram in the hospital, they might have thought there was no rush." He shrugged, but he suddenly became very aware of the woman beside him, the dark and her scent, her smile and her softness. His heart thumped.

"Let's try this one." He moved down the hall a couple of paces. No toys, but the bed in it was stripped, too.

He shut the light off and closed the door. A streetlight from outside shone in through the window and glowed in her hair. Her upturned face held a question, and he read something more in the parting of her lips and her quick breaths.

He schooled his own features and willed his breathing to deepen and slow. He wanted to touch her cheek, slide his hand through her hair, but he hooked it around his neck instead. "I guess I'll stay here on the couch tonight, and you can head to the farmhouse."

"I guess," she said softly.

Her scent, sweet and sassy, feminine and confident, swept past his nose. She leaned forward; her hand landed on his chest. "Ben..."

He put his own hand over hers, trying hard to remember it was just yesterday when he wasn't good enough for her to introduce him to her dad as her man.

He swallowed, and the sound seemed loud in the silence that stretched between them. "I made Eve text me last night when you got home. I wanted to make sure you got there okay." His voice came out deep and soft, with jagged edges. "Should I have her do it again tonight, or will you let me know?"

Her fingers curled slightly into his chest, and each pressure point burned like fire and ice. He gritted his teeth against the torture.

"I've been going home by myself for years, and no one has checked up on me."

He whispered low, "I want to take care of you."

"It scares me that I want to let you." Her actions belied her words because she leaned even closer. Her tongue came out and touched her lips. He released a harsh breath at the sight.

Taking his hand from his neck, he slowly slipped it behind her head, into her hair, threading his fingers through the fine strands like he'd wanted to do for days.

"I can't remember anyone ever taking care of me." Her hand slid around his chest to his back.

"You can make new memories with me." He put his other hand around her and pulled her closer until their bodies touched. If flames had erupted between them, he wouldn't have been surprised.

"I can't. I'm the only one that's ever been there for me. I can't lean on you. You're not even pretending to plan to stay."

"Riley, I'd..." He closed his mouth. It had been on the tip of his tongue to tell her that he wanted to stay. To forget the six-month limit. That he wanted to be with her forever.

He almost groaned aloud. But she'd made it clear that she was doing what her dad wanted and what was best for the company.

She doesn't want you, fool. How many times does she have to say it?

He closed his eyes for a brief second before stepping back. "Text me, please."

"I will."

He dropped his hands, and she moved away immediately, out into the dining room and, a few seconds later, out the door. Her car started, and she was gone. He hadn't moved.

He could grab a few blankets and pillows and sleep on the couch. It would be comfortable, but he wasn't going to sleep. Not for a while. Holding Riley had been even better than he'd imagined. And he'd imagined it a lot. His hands fisted, wishing she were still under them.

Was there anything he could do to change her mind?

He supposed he could take four years and get a college degree. But he'd still be poor. He needed to be educated and rich.

Walking outside, he sat on the top step of the little porch, leaning against the side of the trailer with his leg bent and his head tilted back to look at the stars.

It was then that he remembered the paper Tough had given him early that morning. He'd folded it and stuffed it into his back pocket. He'd shifted it into these jeans when he changed then promptly forgotten about it.

Did he even want to know?

A cool breeze blew across the grass, and the scent of a summer evening filled him with nostalgia. His childhood had ended early. And ever since he'd been working to help his mom and raise his sisters. But, he supposed to a man like Mr. Coleman, what Ben had done with his life wasn't worth much.

Ben resolved to not be sad for the years that had passed. He'd done his best. And would keep doing his best. Wasn't that the measure of a man? What he did when no one was watching? When he didn't expect a reward or accolades. No one was going to thank him for raising his sisters and doing his best for them. He'd known that when he started, and he knew it now.

He wasn't going to live for what other people thought. He was going to do right, no matter who saw him and even if no one ever noticed.

Maybe that meant that Riley would never be with him. As much as that thought pained him, he couldn't dismiss it. He wasn't going to quit being the best mechanic he could be, just so he could pay someone to let him spend four years earning a worthless piece of paper to impress Mr. Coleman.

He reached into his back pocket. Working with Tough today had impressed Ben. He was a good man. Humble. With a discerning eye that didn't miss much. What would he have to say?

Ben opened the paper. It crackled as he stretched it out and tilted it toward the streetlight. There wasn't much on it. Just one line.

Tell Riley you love her.

Yeah, well, Tough had seen right through his "made-up" story.

At least he didn't have to worry about Tough telling anyone.

Chapter Seventeen

Monday morning, Ben woke without an alarm. Funny how the older he got, the less he seemed to be able to sleep. Or maybe he just had more interesting things to think about. Whatever it was, he got up and showered. It had been a long afternoon with Gram yesterday. She was used to being active and didn't make a very good patient. It wasn't that she wasn't allowed to move. She just wasn't allowed to move as much as she was used to.

That and she couldn't eat steak. Or bacon.

Still, Riley and the twins had come, and they'd spent most of the day on lawn chairs in the backyard until Turbo and Harris had come in the evening to relieve them.

While sitting there in the long afternoon, he'd had an idea about something he could do in the yard here at the farmhouse. He kind of wanted to surprise Riley with it, but since it wasn't his house, he'd probably better get permission first. Then the saying, "It's easier to get forgiveness than permission," ran through his head, and he figured, what could it hurt?

Riley had mentioned a business trip next week. He'd think about doing it then.

When he looked out the door, the eastern sky was just starting to glow, and Riley was at the rail, waiting on him.

He hadn't been sure she'd be there. After all, he was the one who had quit with their little early morning meetings Saturday morning when he'd been angry. Although she's the one that said she was quitting.

It was nice she forgave him so easily.

Her head turned when he opened the door and stepped out still in his bare feet. Her eyes crinkled, and her smile hit him straight in the gut. Maybe he was foolish to come out and expose his heart.

"Good morning, Ben," she said softly.

"Morning." He walked slowly to her. Their eyes held as he walked to the rail beside her. He didn't put his arms around her like he'd longed to do all night. Would she lean into him like she did at the hospital? Or like she had in Gram's hall? He was willing to take the chance, but he didn't want to push Riley.

He breathed in the scent he would forever associate with sweet happiness.

They didn't talk a lot. The sunrise touched their faces, turning them pink then orange along with the wide expanse of sky over the low mountain bench in the distance. Somehow this morning he was aware of every breath she took, every time the slight breeze took her hair and shifted it. He wanted to touch her skin, feel her heart against his, but he reminded himself it wasn't his right.

He had his eyes on the sky, trying to focus on the beauty before him, his forearms resting on the banister, his hands clasped, when her fingertips touched his arm. He almost jumped out of his skin from the charge. His eyes snapped to hers, but she was looking at the flaming sky, as though in awe. Her light touch scrambled his brain and made the sunset pale in comparison to the feelings that stirred in his soul.

Pretty sure that wasn't part of the fake marriage bargain. Whatever was going on between them, he hoped he'd be able to stand it when it ended.

～

"Tell me again why there's such a rush in finishing this?" Torque thumped the brick that Jamal handed him down in the flat layer of sand. He shifted it slightly then looked at Ben.

Ben shrugged. "You don't have to stay."

"Thinking your ears need cleaning, man. Didn't say I didn't want to stay." He held his hand out for the next brick that Jamal set in his hand. "I asked what the rush was."

Ben took the other brick Jamal handed him. He should have worn gloves. He'd already smashed the pointer finger on his left hand. It wasn't bleeding out the cracked nail anymore, but it still throbbed.

He set his brick before he answered Torque. "I wanted to surprise Riley and have it done before she got home."

"She's not coming home until Tuesday. It's Friday night." Torque slid over on his knees and took another brick from Jamal.

Ben slid in the opposite direction. They'd already made the stone fire ring. He'd welded the large three-foot-in-diameter metal inside ring together at the Coleman shop yesterday. It was installed as well. He'd prepared the ground Wednesday night after he'd visited Gram. That's when he'd seen Torque and told him what he was doing. Torque and Jamal had just shown up tonight around seven, straight from work, since they were both just as grease-covered as he was.

Ben knew he didn't really need to answer Torque, but the fact that his brother knew he was working on a project and had come to lend a hand without being asked...it kind of made him feel like he actually had a real family. For the first time since his mother died.

Not that the twins weren't "real," but he was more like a dad to them than a brother.

"I can't just sit around the house while she's gone. I need to be busy."

A flash of white teeth shone in the light of the floodlights.

Jamal laughed. "Dad's the same way, Uncle Ben. He can't sit still when Mom's not home."

A little thrill went through him every time one of his nieces or nephews called him Uncle Ben. Jamal handed him another brick then hurried around to give another one to Torque.

The hardest part was getting the pattern started. At this point, they were almost done, and the bricks went in easily. They would form a nice paving circle around the fire ring. Decorative and also acting as a safety ring for stray sparks.

"You're gonna finish this tonight. Then what're you going to do?" Torque asked, sliding down again then slapping another brick in place.

"I don't know. Maybe if I'm lucky, the toilet will back up, and I'll have to dig the septic system up."

Torque snorted. He looked at Jamal. "If that happens, we're busy."

Jamal chuckled again. His voice was cracking a little. He was right at that point where he sounded like a little boy most of the time, with occasional flashes of the deepened man's voice he'd have next year this time. "Whatever, Dad. All your brothers have to do is say they're doing something, and you're there helping."

Torque didn't say anything else, but Ben felt that familiar warmth spreading in his chest. He was one of the brothers. He'd come in, after being gone for years, running away, avoiding his family because of his dad, and yet they'd accepted him without question.

The back door slammed, and Cassidy walked out, a black-haired twin walking on either side of her.

"Yes!" Jamal said. "She's got drinks."

"I think your sisters are carrying cookies." Torque's eyes lingered on his wife. He looked at Cassidy the way Ben wanted to look at Riley. "I heard you pull in."

Ben had heard the car too, but he'd assumed it was one of the caretakers. Torque would recognize the sound of his wife's car.

"I set some food on the counter." She bent down and kissed her husband before handing him a bottle of water. Torque tossed it over the fire ring, and Ben caught it.

"Thanks."

He jerked his head as a twin wiggled into each arm.

Cassidy said, "You're welcome. This looks amazing. You guys are coming over to our house next week to put one in there, right?"

"Maybe the next week. I think Ben's doing some plumbing first." One side of Torque's mouth pulled up.

Ben grunted.

"Okay." Cassidy looked between them. "Inside joke?"

"It probably depends if Aunt Riley goes away again. Uncle Ben is the same as Dad when you aren't home."

"Oh? So, he put the spice rack in alphabetical order and moved Riley's makeup to the basement so he could put a toolbox the size of South Dakota under the bathroom sink?" Cassidy asked with a quirked brow.

"I didn't touch the spice rack." Ben put both hands in the air in innocence.

"Hmm." Cassidy put a hand on her hip.

"I did not put your makeup in the basement," Torque said as the twins crawled over him.

"That's only because I caught you as you were coming down the stairs with it."

Torque looked over at Ben. "Don't ever touch your wife's makeup."

This probably wasn't the time to confess that he'd never been in his wife's bathroom. "Noted."

"The other day when I was talking to Riley, she said she didn't know if you two were staying here in Pennsylvania." Cassidy plucked a twin off Torque so he could drink his water.

"Yeah. We're not real sure what we're going to do." Ben met Cassidy's gaze. It was the first time since the sun went down that he wished the floodlights weren't so bright.

"Obviously it's up to you and what's best for you guys, but I know your brothers would love for you to come back to PA and stay."

"She's right." Torque spoke, surprising Ben. "I guess I spent a lot of years angry that you left. We didn't know you had a mother in Maine. After getting to know you and Riley, at the very least, we'd like to stay in touch."

Ben studied the cap he held between his fingers. In order for his deceit to work, he had to disappear after they'd finished their work here. When he'd made his bargain with Riley, he'd never dreamed he'd actually like his brothers or want to be part of their lives. Everything had changed.

He looked up and met Torque's brown eyes—eyes just like his own —across the fire ring. "I'd like that too." It was an honest answer.

Chapter Eighteen

Ben sat back on his haunches, surveying his handiwork. Finally finished. Cassidy had left shortly after she'd come, taking the twins. Torque and Jamal had headed out an hour ago when all that was left to do was spread the sand in the cracks. He would have stayed until it was completely done, but Ben had sent him home to his wife.

He grabbed his water bottle and took a swig. It felt more like six months than three days that Riley had been gone.

Thankfully he had a truck coming in tomorrow for a rebuild and would spend the rest of the weekend on it, working late both nights. He appreciated Torque coming because whatever he hadn't gotten done tonight would have had to wait. But he'd finished it, so he would get to surprise Riley after all.

Eight hours on Wednesday night. Eight last night and six tonight. The perfect circle with an inner circular steel core, outer stone sides, and a four-foot-wide brick circular floor around it was finished.

It had been a good idea, since he wasn't sleeping much anyway with her gone. Funny how short of a time it took for him to get used to watching the sun come up with her and eating breakfast with her and driving to work with her. Driving home. Cooking supper. Sitting on the porch swing and watching the sun go down.

It was a little unbelievable how much he missed her. He took another swig of his water.

Eve and Eden had decided to finish this semester of classes, at least, which was only another month or so, and come down for the summer. Now they could sit beside the stone fire ring. They could even cook supper over the fire. Gram would love it, and all the nieces and nephews would have a great time.

He laughed to himself. He needed a swing set to make it good for the nieces and nephews.

But he hoped Riley would love it. Maybe he should have asked before making such a drastic change to her backyard, but he'd broached the subject in a generic way, and she'd seemed open to the idea.

A little wave of anxiety went through him. If she didn't like it...

He supposed he could always take it out.

He sighed and finished off his water. Tired, but not sleepy, he knew he'd just go upstairs and toss and turn. Riley had texted him every night when she got back to her family's house where she was staying, but she hadn't texted tonight.

Whether that meant she forgot, or whether that meant she was still out, he didn't know and couldn't think about. He'd really go crazy if he had to try to imagine what Riley might be doing running around at midnight. Now that his hands were no longer busy, it was even worse.

He got to his feet, shoving his hands in his pockets and walking over to the side of the porch, leaning against it.

Why hadn't she texted?

Crossing his arms over his chest, he stared off into the night, trying to get his mind to focus on anything other than Riley in a ditch somewhere. Riley attacked by thugs. Riley in the hospital. Riley only taking three days to forget about him when he couldn't stop thinking about her.

The hum reached him first. He cocked his head. Then lights shone by the house. The hum grew closer, and he knew for sure: Riley hadn't texted because she had been on her way home. Thrilled excitement pulsed hot and prickly through his blood.

He waited for the lights to shut off before he walked around the side of the house. Running would be unseemly, but that's what he wanted to do. Hurry to her car door and sweep her up in a big hug and hello kiss.

She popped the trunk, and he went straight back to get her suitcase. She might be his wife, but a hug probably wasn't appropriate, either. Maybe she wasn't home early because she missed him. It could be something else.

He pulled her suitcase and shoulder bag out, slamming the trunk.

"Oh!" Riley said from beside the car. "I wasn't expecting you to be up."

He looked at her. He hadn't even left the front porch light on since he wasn't expecting her home, so the three-quarter moon was the only light. Did she really think he'd go to bed not having heard from her?

"You didn't text."

She smiled. "Because I was coming home."

Irritation sizzled up his spine. Didn't she know he'd want to know that she was safe?

Her smile faded. "I can get that. You don't have to put yourself out because of me."

He ground his teeth together. Like he was going to let her carry the heavy suitcases when he was right here. "I've got them. Just get in the house." She was in his way, and he couldn't walk around the car.

"I'm perfectly capable of carrying my own luggage." She put her hands on her hips. "And maybe I don't want to go in the house."

She wasn't acting the slightest bit happy to see him. In fact, she seemed put out because he was carrying her bags. Of course, he knew she could do it. But he wouldn't feel like a man if he stood and watched her lug her stuff in without helping her. Could she really be that dense? Maybe she was trying to make him feel worthless.

No. Wait. This was Riley. She wasn't mean, and she didn't hate him. Maybe she was tired. He shoved his irritation back. It wasn't considerate of her to not text and let him know she was okay, but it was dumb for him to get upset about it. She wasn't one of the twins. Maybe she really didn't realize that he wouldn't sleep until he was sure she was fine.

He swallowed, striving for a neutral tone. "If you don't feel like going in the house, I did something in the backyard. You can check it out and tell me what you think."

She stopped with her mouth open. It closed. Her aggressive stance melted as her shoulders slumped. "I'm sorry," she said softly. "I was acting like a child just now."

His hand tightened on the handles of her luggage. He breathed in. Her scent filled his lungs. He'd missed it. He'd worried. But he couldn't tell her that. So he acted irritated instead. Then she thought he wasn't happy to see her.

Sometimes he was just stupid. He set her bags down and stepped forward.

Her head jerked up. Her eyes widened as she must have realized his intent.

He moved slow, giving her the chance to step back or to the side. To tell him to stop. But she didn't. She took a half step forward and met him. Their eyes held as he stopped, wrapping his arms around her slim waist, feeling her heat and softness.

It wasn't the first time they'd embraced, but always before it had been for an audience. Except the time in Gram's hall, with Gram being in the bedroom close by.

This time, they were alone.

She stiffened, and his heart cramped before she melted against him. Her arms slipped around his waist. He trembled at the soft touch. She squeezed. He closed his eyes, resting his cheek on the top of her head.

"I missed you," he said roughly. He forced his mouth to open. "I was worried about you when you didn't text." His whole chest constricted, trying to keep the next words in, but they came out anyway, raw and rough. "I couldn't figure out what you'd be doing running around Richmond at midnight. If you were hurt. If you were...with someone."

She froze in his arms. Then she pulled back just enough to throw her left hand in the air, twisting it so her grandmother's ring caught the moonbeams. "I'm a married woman." She lifted her face, staring into his eyes.

"No one that you work with knows that," he said around the weight in his chest.

"I'm sorry you worried. I'm sorry I didn't text." She pulled her lips in, her eyes heavy with contrition. "I shoved all my meetings into the past three days because driving away from...here...was harder than I thought it would be, and every second I was gone, I longed to be back."

His heart beat heavy. "That's why you're home early?"

"Yes."

"Because you missed...here?"

"No," she whispered. "I missed *you*."

Their gazes held. A cool breeze blew, blowing strands of her hair across his forearm. Her body felt warm and alive under his hands.

He didn't know what it meant or where they were going in their odd relationship. But he did know that he felt the world had been set back to rights, now that Riley was in his arms.

He pulled her close again, loving the way she came so easily, pressing into him. He didn't want to let her go, to try to untangle the convoluted mess of their relationship. But she had to be tired. "Let me carry your things in." He quickly added, "I know you can do it. But it makes me feel good to do it for you."

She grunted. He considered that a win.

"Then I'll show you what I did in the backyard."

"Okay," she said, her cheek still pressed against his chest, like she didn't want to let go any more than he did.

Again, he wasn't sure what it meant. But he liked it.

Chapter Nineteen

onday afternoon, Riley sat at her desk with her head in her hands. Trying to organize all the scattered paperwork had turned out to be a real nightmare. She couldn't believe how convoluted the person before her had been in their record-keeping. No wonder this terminal didn't perform to its potential. She'd sat in on a staff meeting first thing this morning and had spent the next six hours working on unwinding the electronic records.

She stretched and stood. It was time for a break. Ben had texted that he was working through lunch, so she'd not seen him since this morning.

Smiling at the memory of watching the sun come up with him, laughing a little more at the way his big body had jerked when she'd touched his arm again, she felt immensely lighter.

She stopped at the cafeteria and grabbed a sandwich and water for them both before heading over to the shop. Her dad was gone, visiting their terminal in Virginia. He wouldn't be back until next week.

Her stride hitched a little when she walked into the shop. The first shift guys were gone. Second shift was not as busy. She nodded to several guys she recognized, but her eyes kept going back to the woman's boots which stuck out from under the truck that was parked in Ben's bay.

Ben's boots were right beside hers. Neither one of their torsos was visible, hidden by the big steer tire and motor.

Riley forced her feet to keep moving. She'd been enjoying time with Ben, but they weren't really married. There was no exclusive agreement between them whatsoever. This pressure in her chest was uncalled for.

"I didn't realize you could do it that way." The woman's voice drifted out from under the truck.

Ben grunted.

Some clanging and sharp bangs sounded. Ben's feet moved like he was exerting pressure.

"Oh, here. Let me." The woman's voice came again.

Riley tried to remember the woman's name. She'd seen it on the shop reports. Fran. She was pretty sure that was it.

Suddenly Ben's body shot into sight, like he'd grabbed the truck and pushed off in frustration. The thunderclouds in his eyes eased as he saw Riley. He sat up, a wrench in one hand, the other hand running through his hair.

Get rid of her, please, he mouthed.

With pleasure, Riley mouthed back.

The woman slid out. Her jeans were tight. Her t-shirt tighter. "Why'd you leave?" she pouted. Her expression changed as she caught sight of Riley.

Riley smiled. "Hi, Fran. I'm here to do a spot inspection, and your number came up. Can you take me to your workstation and show me your daily maintenance and equipment log, please?"

The woman's brows drew down, and her lips pushed out. "I thought Ben did the inspections."

"I'm Ben's boss, and I report to the company owner. Inspections are Ben's job and my responsibility. Lead on, please."

Ben mouthed, "Thank you," as she followed Fran to the other end of the shop. Riley held the sandwiches and drinks up as she walked away. Ben jerked his head in acknowledgment with a grin.

Twenty-five minutes later, Riley was back. Ben had a cracked air to air lying beside the truck, his boots sticking out as he lay on the creeper, and Riley could only assume he was under there putting the new one on.

Riley looked down through the frame rails. "If you need help, I can get Fran to come on back."

"And I can go lie down on the hammer lane of the closest interstate."

"Please, no. I need you."

Ben grunted and slid out. "Not 'Ben, I like you and don't want to see anything happen to you.' Nope. I get 'turn the company around first, then jump off a bridge.'"

"You're fishing for a compliment? I'd have thought you'd have your ego stroked with Fran down here lying under the truck with you." She handed him a sandwich and water.

"I know it's often the other way around. Men harassing women. I've seen it, but man, I wish she'd find someone else to bother. I spent half my time today running from her." He took the lid off and took a deep drink.

"Looked like she caught you when I walked in."

"I was sick of not getting anything done."

"I can transfer her."

"I can too." He lifted a brow at her. She tilted her head to acknowledge the truth in his words. Officially, he wasn't allowed to deal directly with employee movement. Unofficially, she'd bowed to his decisions for years. How was she to know who worked well and who didn't?

"I ran the numbers for last week. We're already seeing improvement here."

"Here?"

She sighed. "Yeah. Here in the shop. Upstairs, not so much."

"What's up?" He took a bite of the sandwich.

"Just still trying to untangle the records mess."

"That bad?"

"It's worse."

"It's looking good here. I've got a few things I want to implement, but I'm waiting until I've been here a bit and people have accepted me."

Riley nodded. It was technically against company policy for a supervisor to do the work of a mechanic, but the guys accepted him a lot easier and faster if he worked. Not to mention it made sense.

"You've never had a problem with people liking you."

He shrugged. "Guys respect a hard worker. I found it out by accident back when I didn't had a choice about working hard."

Riley nodded. It had become part of his character.

He changed the subject. "I have two trucks sitting down there that could be fixed and on the road, except we're out of the parts I need, which we should have known and they should have been automatically ordered, but the parts aren't being checked out. That's definitely a time-waster that needs to be changed immediately."

Riley's brain was calculating. "You need a whole new system?"

"No," he said firmly. "The computer system is great. I need the guys to use it properly. Some guys forget to check their parts out. Which also means that we're not getting paid for them if it's an outside job."

"I see."

"Right. Anyway, I know exactly how I'm going to take care of it, I just don't want to rock the boat too soon."

"Yep. That gets people upset."

They finished their sandwiches in silence.

"What time are you quitting today?" Riley asked.

He crossed his arms over his chest and leaned back against the drives. "I can quit anytime. This truck's done. I have one coming in on the hook, needs to be rebuilt, but night shift can steam it off." He looked her in the eye. "I think we can get rid of night shift, to be honest."

"Really?" Her eyes widened. That would be a big savings.

"We might have to have some second shift guys stay or cover occasionally, and maybe we'd need to reinstitute it if other shops' work got dumped on us like we did in Maine, but for now, it would solve the employee shortage. Nothing much gets done at night anyway."

"No supervision."

"Basically."

She looked down, picking at her nail.

"I'm ready to go whenever you are. Just give me a fifteen-minute heads-up to clean up my tools and wash up."

Her face broke out in a smile. The heat from his seeped into her bones.

She balled up her trash and finished her water. "Let me know if you need me to rescue you from Fran again."

"I have plans for Fran. I just have to implement them slowly. She's going to be part of the big shake-up."

They smiled together. "I'm going to work another couple of hours. Maybe cut out at six?"

"Perfect. I'd like to visit Gram."

"Of course."

Chapter Twenty

R iley had texted Ben and let him know she wasn't going to be able to quit, and if he wanted to see his gram before she went to bed, he'd need to leave without her.

He was glad he did, because all three of his brothers were outside with their wives and children when Eve and Eden and he pulled in. The trailer's backyard wasn't very big, but there was a small swing set for the kids.

Gram was set up in a lawn chair, a blanket tucked around her legs even though it wasn't cold out.

"She looks like a queen holding court," Eve said as they walked back.

That was true. Ben's heart tugged in his chest. Harris sat in a lawn chair beside Gram, one hand on the gentle swell of her belly. Turbo was sprawled at her feet. Occasionally one of Torque's twins would come over and jump on him, and he'd wrestle easily with them.

Torque sat on the ground facing Gram, Cassidy leaned back between his legs, watching the kids and laughing, his arms around her.

Tough lay on his side, one hand propping his head up, his body curved around Kelly who sat on the ground and leaned against his stomach.

"There's Ben and the twins," Turbo called out. "Come on over. We're out of lawn chairs, so you'll have to find a spot on the ground."

Eve and Eden walked over and kissed Gram on the forehead before heading to the swing set to push Torque and Cassidy's dark-haired twins. Ben sat on the ground, leaning back on his hands. He couldn't quite meet Tough's eyes. He'd thrown the note on his dresser but hadn't seen Tough much since. He couldn't believe that Tough had seen right through everything.

"Where's Riley?" Cassidy asked.

"She got caught up in some work at the terminal and told me to come without her." He hadn't realized how much he wanted a wife— not just any wife, but Riley—until he'd started spending time with her. But seeing his brothers and their wives together made the longing so much worse. Why couldn't he have that happiness? Not that he begrudged it of his brothers. He certainly didn't. After the childhood they'd all had, he deserved to be happy.

"How are you feeling today, Gram?"

"Like I'm sick and tired of being sick and tired," she said with a snap in her voice. Ben grinned. She hadn't lost her spark.

The talk turned to shop, and Ben enjoyed the easy camaraderie of men who worked with their hands for a living.

He'd been there an hour and dusk had fallen when a car pulled in. From his position, he could only see headlights, but he was talking to Torque about fuel-to-air ratios in the new CAT engines, and since he wasn't expecting anyone, he didn't pay much attention. Not even when his sisters hurried past to greet the newcomer.

Then Riley walked around the corner of the trailer, Eve and Eden on either side of her, their arms around her narrow waist.

Ben's heart stopped, and longing ripped through his chest. What if their marriage were real? He closed his eyes. He had to stop thinking like that. Just because his little brothers all were happy in their marriages didn't mean that he needed the same thing.

He opened his eyes to find Riley's gaze sweeping across the yard, taking in the domestic couples sprawled on the ground, the kids on the swing set and playing in the sand, and Gram in her chair. Lastly, her eyes rested on him. She smiled, and his heart catapulted straight up into the sky. He didn't move. He didn't trust himself to not get up and go right to her and take her in his arms.

"Hey, everyone," Riley said. She moved away from the twins and bent down to kiss Gram on the cheek. "How are you doing, Gram?"

Ben listened to her talk, his heart thumping in his chest. Where was she going to sit? If the couples weren't arranged the way they were, it wouldn't be a big deal. But if they were the only couple that wasn't together, it would be obvious.

Ben leaned his head back, looking up at the stars that were just starting to shine. He turned his head. Tough stared at him. When Ben met his gaze, his brow moved a fraction of an inch. Whatever that was supposed to mean.

Maybe a reminder that he was supposed to tell Riley he loved her. Like he even knew what love was. He hadn't seen much of it in his life. His sisters and his mom.

Loving his mom had hurt. Loving his sisters had meant a lot of tough decisions. Neither scenario was how he felt toward Riley.

Something brushed one of his raised knees. A moment later, Riley settled between his legs, her posture confident. Only he could see the insecurity on her face as she waited to see his reaction.

His whole body buzzed and ached. He'd wanted this for so long. Even if his entire family was watching, he would still savor and enjoy finally holding her close.

He sat up and wrapped her in his arms, nuzzling her ear. "Thank you," he said, gratitude flowing like a river in flood stage through his chest.

"I'm sorry," she whispered back. "I didn't realize it was a couples' thing tonight." She turned her head so their lips were almost touching. He breathed her air.

"It didn't matter." But he lied.

"You shouldn't be alone."

"I'm not."

She smiled.

"You guys are acting like newlyweds, all whispery," Turbo said.
Eve choked.
Eden cleared her throat. "They're always like that."

Ben's eyes shot to her. When did she become such a good liar?

He felt Tough's eyes on him again. Funny how that brother could say a whole speech with just a look. And even funnier how nothing missed his observation. He turned, just to make sure that Tough wasn't going to rat him out.

No worries there. Tough had a small smile on his face. Ben held his gaze, leaning forward a fraction and kissing Riley on the temple. He returned the small smile.

If it felt this good to hold her, to have her walk over and choose him, how good would it be if she really meant it? If she actually did choose him over everything, including her dad and his company?

Even as he sat there, enjoying the closeness and warmth of Riley, he knew that was the only way he'd ever completely trust her after what she did.

A couple of kids had come over and settled down beside their parents. The adults were chatting soft and low when a rumble vibrated on the ground.

"Sounds like a Harley," Ben said.

A headlight flashed.

"It's Dusty," Torque replied

Some dude on a bike.

Did Riley like motorcycles? Funny that's the first thing that entered his head. He'd wanted a bike back in his twenties, but it wasn't practical with the twins, and he'd never gotten one.

Maybe he'd buy one when he left Riley. A consolation of sorts. But until then, he was going to enjoy every moment with her, memorizing the feeling of not being alone anymore.

The bike pulled up to the edge of the trailer and shut off. Ben glanced over at it—some skinny guy in black leather sat on it, feet braced on each side. He turned back to Riley, gauging her reaction. If he bought a bike now, they could ride around together for the rest of the summer and fall. They couldn't talk like in a car, but she'd be snuggled up against him every day.

But her brows were drawn together, and her eyes narrowed slightly.

He nuzzled her ear. "I love that look."

She stiffened. "Yeah, most guys do."

He pulled back at her annoyed tone, ignoring the greetings of the adults around them. "Huh?"

She was looking in the direction of the bike but cut her eyes to his. "The girl-biker look. You didn't have to tell me. Most guys dig it."

Ben's eyes narrowed. He glanced over at the Harley. Sure enough, the slender boy had taken his helmet off, revealing long blond hair and delicate facial features. "That's a girl."

"You keep stating the obvious..." Riley tilted her head. "You weren't talking about Dusty?"

"That she's a girl? Yeah." He was missing something. But he couldn't figure out what.

"That you love the blond-on-a-bike look, taking her helmet off and shaking her hair out."

Oh, she thought he'd been talking about Dusty. "Missed it. I was looking at this." He used one finger to stroke the lines between her eyes. "You look like that at work sometimes when you're trying to figure out a really tough problem. It's that super-intelligent woman look that really drives me crazy." He hadn't meant to let all that come tumbling out of his mouth, but it was too late.

Riley smiled. "You really weren't looking at her."

"I don't know why you find that so hard to believe. There's only one woman I've ever been interested in looking at." And that *really* wasn't supposed to come out, either.

She stared into his eyes, and he couldn't look away, like their gazes had been welded together. The sounds around them faded away, and he hung on her every breath, waiting to see what she'd do with his declaration. Would she brush it off? Would she make one of her own?

"Ben, Riley, I don't think you've ever met Dusty." Turbo stretched out a booted toe and nudged Ben's knee, effectively breaking the spell between them.

"No, we haven't," Ben said, reluctantly moving to stand.

"Don't get up," Dusty said, with her hand out. Ben liked that she held it out to Riley first and spoke to her. "You two look too cozy down there to move."

"I feel too cozy to move," Riley said, her smile genuine. She shook Dusty's hand. "It's great to meet you."

"It's nice to meet you too." Dusty's blond hair contrasted with her black leather jacket.

Ben reluctantly took his hand away from Riley to shake Dusty's. The callouses on her palm surprised him a little. That's when he noticed the slight droop of her eyes. Despite her smile, she seemed sad. Maybe she felt the same way he had when he walked back, alone, into all the happy couples.

Dusty moved on, and Ben tucked his arm back around Riley.

"That's the kind of girl I'd always pictured you with."

"Funny, since I could never picture you with anyone but me."

She snorted like he'd made a joke, and he was a little glad she took it that way, although he hadn't meant it as a joke.

"I'm serious," she said. "Dusty rides a Harley for goodness' sake."

"So?"

"Isn't that something you're interested in?"

"Owning a Harley? Maybe someday."

"No, goofy. A girl that does."

It was like she was trying to push him away. Or push him toward Dusty. Either one. His heart hurt. Did she feel like he was getting too close? Too serious? He'd said more from his heart tonight than he'd ever said before.

He needed to back off.

The next day, Riley drove them to work since she had a business lunch to attend. Ben had been quiet and a little more aloof than usual, although they'd still watched the sunrise together. This time, they'd sat on the steps together, and he'd held her. She'd been more content than she could ever remember being, snuggled in his arms.

But it was like he'd realized yesterday that maybe he would be interested in a girl like Dusty. Or maybe in Dusty herself.

She was afraid to ask.

She dropped him off at the back of the garage before driving around and parking in her usual spot. Resting her hands on the wheel, she didn't get out right away. Sometime between last night and this morning, she realized that she was in love with Ben Baxter. Completely, head over heels, blindly in love with him

It started with the absolute, unreasonable jealousy that had erupted in her soul—for no reason—when she'd seen Dusty. Ben wasn't even looking at her. Didn't spend more than five seconds talking to her. Yet, Riley had been unreasonably jealous for the first time in her life.

And why not? Ben was amazing in every way.

Riley grabbed her briefcase and got out of her car. She should tell Ben. But she couldn't. As she opened the door to the building using her key, she listed the reasons in her head.

First of all, she was his boss. A relationship with a subordinate would be all kinds of wrong.

Secondly, her dad had been clear. Everything she'd been working for her whole life was on the line. If he found out that she and Ben were together, she could lose everything.

Would that be so horrible?

She stopped short, her finger reaching for the elevator button.

Wouldn't having Ben be better than a corner office and her dad's approval? She could hardly believe she was thinking this way. It had never crossed her mind before. She had always been so focused on work.

The idea was bold and big and new, and she needed time to think about it. Before she could act on anything, though, she needed to do her part to turn this terminal around.

Chapter Twenty-One

The weeks went by, Gram slowly mended, the twins went back to Maine to pick up where they'd left off, and Ben and Riley settled into a routine. Watching the sunrise together in the morning. Going their separate ways at work—Riley approving every change Ben made and trying to unwind her own issues in the office. Slowly the terminal was turning.

They cooked supper together in the evening and often sat outside by the fire ring that Ben had made the week she was gone to meet with her dad at their Virginia facility. Easy friendship lay soft, like a spring rain, between them, but the attraction that had always marked their relationship was not dormant. Not for her.

But she didn't talk about it, didn't acknowledge it, and neither did he. Since the night when he'd told her he couldn't imagine her with any man but him, he'd pulled way back. It was like they'd never been close. She should have been relieved, since that was the night that she realized she was in love with Ben. Completely, head over heels in love with Ben. It had scared her. He would never want to actually be with a girl like her. Someone like Dusty was much more his style. Thankfully, he'd seemed to realize it when she pointed it out and gotten quiet before she said something stupid like she'd wanted to many times over the past few weeks. Something like, "How about we be married for real?"

She just needed to keep it together for another six weeks.

By unspoken agreement, they'd not spent much time together when they were at work. Her dad hadn't asked for another tour, and they'd accomplished what she had barely even hoped to accomplish—his family believed they were happily married, and her dad didn't even know they were on speaking terms. Her mom was a nonissue. Although she'd broken up with husband number five and now had a penthouse in New York City with her new boyfriend.

Riley clicked a few more keys on her office computer. This one sticky issue of figuring out the information filing system had taken up a majority of her time since she'd started, and she almost had it all figured out. The one huge hang-up had been eight missing IFTA reports. She would need them when the insurance renewed in three months, and she still hadn't found them, even though she'd been through every folder on the system a half-dozen times.

Standing, she stretched her back and neck. She walked over to the window where she could see the big garage doors open. It was the wrong angle to see Ben's bay, but it was a comfort to know that he was down there. Their time was almost up, and she didn't want to think about losing him. Her eyes dropped. She hadn't spent much time loafing in her office, but she walked over now to the small loveseat against the far wall. If she moved it against the other wall, she could move her desk so it faced out the window. It was kind of untraditional to have her desk not facing the door, but it wouldn't hurt to try it, right?

She gave the loveseat an experimental push. It moved easily. It would be easy... Her eyes landed on a folder on the floor, just peeking out from where the loveseat had been.

Drawing her brows together, she squatted down. Pulling on it, she realized there were a pile of folders. She picked up the top one. IFTA, it said across the top in big letters. Her heart started racing, and she couldn't contain her smile.

She reached for the other folders, checking under the loveseat to be sure she got them all. Profit and Loss by Department. Records of Employee Performance. All dated in the past year. She laughed and clutched them to her chest. The last supervisor had not been a big computer person. That had been obvious. Apparently, they'd been more comfortable with hard copies. But there were no filing cabinets, so... under the loveseat they'd gone.

She strode over to her desk and sat down, flipping through them to be sure. Yes. All the reports she'd been missing. All the information she needed to make profitable changes. Everything. All here.

So excited she couldn't sit still, she jumped back up and strode to the window. Ben leaned in the opening of one of the big garage doors, a sandwich in one hand, staring in her direction. Another fellow stood beside him, holding a bottle of soda, and a third seemed to be telling a story since his hands were gesturing everywhere, despite the fact that he was holding a bag of potato chips.

They must be taking a late lunch. Riley calculated quickly—her dad had spent the last week in Maine. That terminal had been struggling since Ben and she had left. He was driving back tomorrow. She grabbed her phone and texted Ben.

> Great news!! Can you meet me in the back parking lot?

She held her phone in her hand and watched as he pulled his out of his pocket, read it, and texted back. He put the last bite of his sandwich in his mouth and pushed off from the garage door.

Her phone buzzed.

> Be there in five.

A new clenching gripped her stomach, and her excitement went beyond finding the folders. Even beyond the almost-certainty that she would have the terminal sitting at the top of the company when her dad's investors showed up in a few weeks.

She grabbed her small mirror out of the desk drawer and checked her hair and makeup. Of course, Ben had seen her this morning, and he'd see her again at home, but they didn't usually meet in the middle of the day, and she wanted to look her best.

She hurried out, waving to Jill, and rushed down the hall. The far elevator led directly to the back lot, and she wouldn't see anyone else once she got on.

Pressing the button, she waited impatiently. He would understand her excitement, because he'd lived with her anxiety for the last four and a half months. He'd be happy for her. After all, he'd worked his butt off, staying late, covering shifts, and making every change he could to increase employee production and decrease turnover, which was the biggest problem in the shop.

She stepped out of the elevator and strode right out the doors. Her stride slowed for just a second when she saw how full the lot was and remembered they were painting lines in the regular employee lot and everyone had parked back here this morning. Except her, since she had a special spot out front along with her dad and the chairman of the board.

Then Ben came around the corner, and she forgot everything else, hurrying over to him. He'd washed up; she could see a few drops of water on his face, plus his arms were clean. He'd found a clean t-shirt.

His lips broke into a smile when he saw her excited face, although his brows stayed furrowed like he wasn't sure what he was smiling about but was just happy because she was happy. That was Ben. He'd never once been intimidated by her being his boss or superior. And he'd always done his best to help her. The man had pride, but it didn't get in the way of him wanting everything that was best for her.

She didn't stop until she was right in front of him. "Guess what?"

"You had to have gotten those files straightened out."

"Even better." She didn't mean to, but her hands gripped his biceps. Solid and way too big for her to encircle, she squeezed anyway.

His arms bent, and his muscles rippled under her hands. That, along with him setting his hands on her waist, distracted her for just a second.

Then her smile brightened, and she glowed into his eyes. "I was going to move that loveseat around..."

His smile faded. "I can move it..."

"No, wait." She put a finger on his lips. They could argue about whether or not she was able to move furniture later. "The folders were under it! Everything I've been looking for!"

"Actual folders," Ben said against her finger.

She moved it to the side, where her hand cupped his face, feeling the bristles of his stubble as she'd longed to do for months now.

"Yes! I've mentioned so many times how the person before me wasn't good with computers. Well, they *really* weren't good with computers. They didn't even have the things on the computer. They'd printed everything off." Her arms moved around him, and she hugged him, giving a little hop.

He lifted her and swung her around. "That's great," he said as he set her down. "You have everything you need. You're not working blind anymore, trying to gather the info as you go."

"Nope." She grinned up at him, his face just inches from hers. "We're gonna do this!" She had been so scared they wouldn't pull it off. Without Ben, it wouldn't even be a possibility, but now that she had the records she needed, it was a sure thing.

He grinned down at her, genuinely happy for her. Her body stilled. A new, more potent stirring began deep in her chest.

"I owe you so much," she said.

The excitement of a moment ago changed to heat. The underlying attraction that always pulled at her burst into flames as her eyes searched his. His breath fanned her face, and she became almost hyperaware of his solid back and the feel of his strong hands holding her.

All the memories of the last few months swirled between them. Watching the sun rise wrapped in his arms. Visiting his gram and snuggling with him on the ground. His voice. His laughter. His support. He'd been everything she needed. And he was still here for her. Ready to celebrate. Ready to work harder if she asked.

"Ben, I..." She licked her lips. His eyes dropped, and heat flared in their depths. "I could never repay you for everything you've done."

His chest moved up and down. The pulse in his neck beat erratically. Her own heart seemed to stop and skip and jump.

Her hand moved over his stubble. Her thumb brushed his cheekbone.

"Riley." His voice was low and scratchy, like he'd forced it out, but it also held a warning note.

She ignored it. Staring deep into his eyes, she pressed closer.

He groaned, and his hands clenched in the small of her back.

Her hand slipped around his neck. With her heart trembling, she tugged gently.

He came, like she'd known he would, his head bending toward hers, his eyes, hooded and hot, still searching hers.

His hands stretched out, holding her back before sliding up and burying in her hair.

She rose on her toes and pressed her open lips to his. The heat between them burst into flames, even as his lips stayed soft, careful, like he valued her and cherished the first moments of their first kiss.

She heard a whimper and realized it was her, wanting more than this soft gentleness, wanting Ben to finally need her as much as she needed him.

He growled on the heels of her whimper and gave her what she'd asked for without words. His hands on her back, pressing her to him, lifting her up, the ground beneath them seeming to shake and spin as she lost coherent thought of everything except the man holding her, kissing her, loving her.

"Riley!" Her dad's voice cut into her consciousness. She jerked back as though he'd slapped her, pushing at the same time until Ben loosened his grip and she slid to her feet. Her knees shook, and Ben reached to steady her, his eyes warm and concerned, but she backed away. It felt like a metal weight lodged in her throat as the look on his face changed from tender care to acute realization to pain to closed-off indifference, all in the space of a heartbeat.

She put out her hand and stepped forward. "Ben." She wasn't going to let her dad come between them again. Even if it meant losing her promotion. She would fight for them this time.

But Ben crossed his arms over his chest and stepped to the side, avoiding her hand. His feet planted, ready to face whatever came next. His eyes moved from her to her dad and then beyond.

Riley followed his gaze. Three men came around the corner of the building, walking in from the overflow lot. The investors.

Looking at Ben, her dad spoke low, his face twisted. "I saw you groping her. Unless you want a sexual harassment lawsuit, you'll get your sorry butt back to the garage and stay there. My daughter would never be interested in the likes of you. There's a billionaire coming around the corner that wants to treat her to dinner tonight. Unless you think you can do better than that, scram."

Ben kept his arms crossed and stared over her dad's shoulder. He didn't answer. Maybe he was waiting for her to defend him.

She opened her mouth to protest, but her dad's lasered attention turned to her. "The future of our company depends on these men. If you haven't done what I asked you to do, they're getting your spot. If you have, you'll not only impress me, you'll impress them as well. They've got several interesting proposals." The men had seen them and shifted course. Her dad glanced over and lowered his voice even more. "If you screw this up for me because of some crass affair with a dirty mechanic, you can kiss your future in this company goodbye."

Her eyes got big. They flew from her dad to the men approaching and finally to Ben. If she fought with her dad right now about Ben, at the very least the investors would be turned off because of the inner strife in their company. With the amount of money they were talking about, they couldn't afford to show that kind of weakness.

She glanced at Ben. His face didn't give a clue as to what he was thinking, but he had to realize the implications of this. It wasn't like she hadn't been talking to him about this all summer. Just because the investors being here was a surprise didn't mean that it was any less important.

Summoning her businesswoman façade, Riley squared her shoulders. "This company has never lost business because of me."

Her dad gave her a look before nodding at Ben. "You tried to throw it all away for him once. I don't understand why you can't see all he wants is your money." Directing his words at Ben, he said, "Someone like you is easily replaced. Find another company and try working your tricks there."

"That's not the way it is..."

Her dad threw up a hand, stopping her from speaking.

Ben opened his mouth. "I promised Riley I'd work for another six weeks. Then I'm done." Ben's blank eyes looked at Riley. "You can consider this my notice."

Her dad crossed his arms over his chest, his expression satisfied. He nodded once. "Get back to the garage. We've got business to take care of."

The investors were close enough that Riley didn't have time to say more. Ben turned without looking at her and strode off.

Chapter Twenty-Two

"You have to do what you said you were going to do." Angelina's hands kept pushing her quilting needle in and out of colorful green and red fabric. She shook her head. "I can't believe some people are so rotten."

"It doesn't matter how bad people treat you. You need to be nice anyway." Miss Beulah had long since put her quilting down.

Ben wasn't sure exactly how he'd gotten in the position he was in—sandwiched in a chair between Miss Beulah and Miss Alda in the back corner of Torque's garage. Which, apparently, was the meeting place for the Kicking Quilters. Each of them held one of his hands.

He hadn't answered the text Riley sent him that she was going to dinner with the investors.

He'd been tempted to pack his stuff, call a moving service for his toolbox, and head back to Maine.

He hadn't, but he was too restless to sit still. So he'd ended up at Torque's garage. Torque was changing an airbag on the back drive of a nice Pete, but somehow Ben had gotten kidnapped by the ladies. Which, he supposed, was okay, since Jamal was doing a great job of helping Torque.

The ladies were telling him only truth, he knew, but it didn't make it any easier to hear.

"Well, you ladies can say what you want, but if that girl can't stand up to her dad and defend this boy here, then she's not worth his time." Miss Alda softened her harsh words with a smile.

"That's where you're wrong, Alda. You've got to respect your parents, no matter what."

"But the woman's over thirty years old!"

"She doesn't have to listen to him. She just has to respect him," Miss Beulah said.

Ben leaned forward, resting his forearms on his legs. They had dragged him over and picked the story out of him with their incessant but well-meaning questions. "I wouldn't want her to disrespect her dad. I *don't* want to disrespect her dad."

"So you get her dad to like you." Miss Beulah poked her needle into the fabric a little harder than necessary.

"Hardly. I've been his top mechanic for twenty years."

"Ben's right. There are just some people you can't impress. And you can't force someone to like you. Riley is going to need to make a decision about who she wants to be with." Miss Alda was just as forceful as Miss Beulah. Ben was kind of glad to have her in his corner.

"Or whether she wants love over prestige," Angelina said thoughtfully.

"Yes. That's the choice. It's not even money. It's prestige." Miss Beulah nodded emphatically.

"But she's been working for this job all her life. It's probably not as much about prestige as it is about the satisfaction of finally working her way to the top." Ben couldn't stop himself from defending her even now. What was wrong with him?

It wouldn't have anything to do with that kiss. Just thinking about it made his hands tighten under the old ladies' gentle patting at the idea of holding Riley. The ladies weren't helping, but they seemed to love fussing over him, and Torque didn't need his help, so he stayed where he was.

"I think love will conquer all," Miss Beulah said, with a dreamy quality in her voice.

No one had said anything about love. He didn't love Riley. He just enjoyed being around her. Loved watching the sunrise with her. Missed her when she wasn't with him. Like tonight. And hurt like heck when she acted like he was worthless in front of her dad.

"I'm not asking her to defy her dad. And I'm not asking her to choose me over him. I just want..." His voice trailed off as Torque came around the side of the truck, the blown airbag in hand.

"She doesn't know how you feel." Torque's eyes were serious. "I know guys don't talk about that stuff."

Torque had spent time in prison. He'd really know how guys weren't in touch with their feminine sides.

"But our women need it sometimes." One corner of his mouth kicked up. "I'd take Tough's advice."

Ben stared at him. Had Tough told him that he'd given Ben advice? Torque's face held no answers. Ben wasn't asking. Whether he knew it or not, the implication was that Tough would know what to do.

Since he'd already been told... But wait.

"She just ditched me today for her dad and the billionaire investors. Treated me like I'm a worthless piece of dirt, and yet I'm supposed to go home and tell her I love her?"

Torque twisted the blown airbag, studying it like he'd never seen one before. Finally he looked up. "If you love her, you should tell her. I don't think what she does should affect what you do."

"That's how you live?"

"Didn't say that. Not saying it's easy. Just saying it's what you should do."

Torque and his ladies didn't know the history. They didn't know how he'd already suffered under Riley's hand and how she'd already rejected him and chose her dad and his company over him. He'd already been through that.

But he'd never told her he loved her.

Did he love her?

~

BEN'S PICKUP was not in the drive when Riley pulled into the house. She'd pleaded a headache and didn't go to the dinner. First time in her life that her dad had lined something up for her to do in the business and she'd not done it. His glowering look would have stopped a freight train, but Riley had left anyway.

The headache was real, but she would have fought through that. Ben was the reason she left. She couldn't stand that he might think that she was choosing her dad over him. She had, but she hadn't wanted to. His work would go down the drain along with hers though. And he knew how much those investors meant to their company. So it wasn't just her dad but the company as well.

When had Ben become more important to her than her dad and the company?

She opened the door and stepped into the quiet house. So much different than walking in with Ben, laughing and talking about their day. Kicking her heels off by the door and walking barefoot into the kitchen to help him start supper before running up and changing.

The old house creaked and settled. She stood in the entryway, looking around fondly. She stayed at this house, not because it was the closest, and not even because it was usually empty. She loved it. Even more now that she had memories here with Ben and Eve and Eden. If she walked away from her dad and his company—if she chose Ben— she'd be giving up this house, too, not that it was even an issue. People were always more important than things.

Her appetite had fled, and she didn't bother going to the kitchen but rather walked slowly up the stairs, stopping at the top and looking toward Ben's room. She'd not been in it since he moved in, respecting his privacy, but the door was cracked, and she stood in the doorway, pushing the door open a little and looking around. His room was taken care of with the same meticulous care he gave his tools and workspace. The bed made. His Bible on the nightstand beside his bed. No clothes on the floor. The dresser bare...except for a folded white piece of paper. The only thing in the whole room that didn't seem like it was tucked in place. It just lay there.

The temptation to walk over and read it was almost overwhelming. Her foot actually picked up off the floor like she was going to walk over.

But she forced it back to the ground. Only allowed herself one last deep breath of his scent. Careful to close the door, leaving it cracked like it had been, she jumped when her phone buzzed.

"Hello?" She walked across the hall and flopped down over her bed.

"Riley, it's Eve. Have you seen Ben?"

"He was at work today. But there were people there, and I didn't leave with him."

"He's not answering his phone, and he always takes our calls."

Visions of his pickup mangled in a car accident flew through her head. She shoved them aside. "Is there a problem?" That would be Ben's first question. He'd want to know if the twins were in trouble.

"No. We were just checking in."

"I can call around to his family and see if anyone has seen him."

"If you don't mind? Maybe we're overreacting." There was a beat of silence on the line. "Ben won't talk to us about you and him, but when he does say something about you, his voice gets all soft...we've been thinking that maybe you and he might get together for real?"

Eden's voice came on the line. "Ben deserves a good woman."

"I agree with that," Riley said, her forehead pressed into her blanket. Unfortunately, she had never treated him the way he deserved.

What if she did?

What if she went today, right now, and did what she should have done all those years ago? But her dad was dining with the investors. She couldn't interrupt their meeting... There she went again. Putting the company ahead of Ben.

Eden spoke again, "I just called Torque on my phone, and he said that Ben was back in the corner of his garage that doesn't have very good service. He's fine. Actually, Torque said he was just leaving to go home, so he should be there any minute."

"Okay. Good to hear." Riley got up off the bed and straightened her suit jacket. "I just remembered something I need to do. I need to go."

"Oh. Okay." Eve sounded a little surprised at her abrupt tone, but they quickly said goodbye.

Riley would have to explain later where she needed to go in such a hurry. She'd be able to tell them how it ended, too.

Grabbing her purse and keys, she ran out to her car and headed in the direction of the nice restaurant her dad always took his guests to. She'd been there a hundred times.

As she turned onto the interstate, she thought she saw Ben's truck. She craned her neck, fairly certain it was him, but she wasn't stopping. She'd talk to him in a bit. It didn't even matter if he didn't want her. She had some things she needed to say to her dad, and they'd waited long enough.

It wasn't ten minutes later that she strode with purpose into the restaurant. No one questioned her as she walked back to their regular table.

Her father sat facing her. His brows twitched, but he kept talking.

She stopped beside the table, her stomach feeling like it was filled with live electric wires. Maybe she shouldn't have waited. Maybe she shouldn't have made such an impulsive decision. But she was here now. And she needed to say what she should have said years ago.

The men started to rise, but she held her hand up. "It's okay. Don't get up. Dad, I have something I need to say to you."

"Unless it pertains to this business meeting and the investors' interests, it will have to wait." Her father dabbed his mouth with a pristine white linen napkin, barely sparing her a glance.

Again, she almost walked away, trained since birth to respect the business and put her own wants and needs aside. But she wouldn't. Not this time.

Her dad glanced up again when she didn't move, and she plunged in. "I love Ben. I've loved him since I met him. All the years we've worked together, he's been a man of integrity and honest compassion. I don't know how he feels, but I'm not putting your interests or the company interests ahead of his feelings anymore. I love you, Dad, and I've been a good, loyal daughter, but I'm not hurting anyone for you ever again."

A fork clanged. The three men at the table with her dad stirred uneasily, but she didn't back down.

Her dad set his napkin down deliberately. "He put you up to this."

She felt a hand come around her waist. Her head jerked around. Ben stared down into her eyes. "I didn't. I never would have."

Her eyes blinked slowly. "How did you know I was here?"

"I saw you getting on the interstate. I turned and followed you." His brows lowered. "You were driving too fast."

She leaned into him, a smile on her face.

She swallowed. "That's part of the reason I..."

He put a finger over her lips. "I love you. I love you more than I care about who you work for or what you do for your dad or his company. And if you choose him, I'll stay where I'm at as long as you're there too."

She shook her head, and his finger fell. "I love you. I'm sorry. I'm so sorry that I allowed other things to come before you. I hurt you with my words and most especially with my actions, and I can see that now. Please forgive me."

"Forgiven." He pulled her tight against him and looked across the table at her dad. "I owe you an apology."

Her dad's mouth flattened while his eyes narrowed.

Before he could open his mouth, she said, "We're married, Dad." Riley couldn't believe how good those words tasted coming out of her mouth. "We've been married since I came to Pennsylvania. I'd like for you to be happy for us, but I understand why you wouldn't be."

"I'm sorry I didn't get permission," Ben added.

"I would never have given it, Baxter," her dad snarled, his lips curling up.

Ben nodded. "I'm asking for forgiveness now."

Her dad opened his mouth to say something. Something unkind from the look on his face, and she cringed. Ben had been through enough. He didn't need to stand here and take the abuse from her dad.

"Baxter?" The investor sitting to the right of her father tilted his head. "You said he was a mechanic for your company, and his name was Baxter?"

Ben nodded. "Ben Baxter."

The investor stood and held his hand out. "We hadn't gotten to that point in our meeting, but," he tapped the folder sitting beside his place, "I made some notes about you in my report. Your name kept coming up, both at the shop in Maine and then here."

Riley's face broke out into a huge grin, and her heart raced.

"According to these papers, you've been instrumental in turning this terminal here in Pennsylvania around. I have some more things I want to check out, but you are the main reason for our visit today."

"What?" Her dad half rose from his chair. "I thought we were discussing investments in the company."

"We'll do that. We said next month. But we've got a company in Mexico that could use a man like Ben."

"And one in China," the older, white-haired man said.

"Another in Germany."

"Basically, we want Ben Baxter. With the amount of money that he's on track to save your company, we'd be fools to not take advantage of his skills."

"Any deal we make with your company will include Ben's services in the bargain."

"You guys can talk about that. I've said what I needed to say, and I've gotten the person I came for, so I'll see ya all later." He looked down at Riley. "You coming with me?"

"I am."

She took a last look at her dad. His face wasn't quite as red as it had been. She really did love him. But she wasn't going to push Ben aside again. Whatever they did with their relationship, her dad didn't get to dictate her actions regarding it.

That was going to be her first question to Ben. Where did they go from here? Were they going to stay married? He'd said he loved her. What, exactly, did that mean?

But as they stepped out of the restaurant, Ben's phone rang. From his expression and tone, it wasn't good.

He wasn't on long. "Gram's back in the hospital. It's not looking good for her. I'm going straight there." He paused, looking down into her eyes. "Are you with me?"

"I am." Like he even needed to ask after the scene in the restaurant.

"You know, I need to confess to my family that you and I weren't married as long as we said we were."

She almost said "why," but she knew immediately what his answer would be. Because he wanted to be honest and not live a lie for the rest of his life.

Especially if they were staying in Pennsylvania. The questions of what was going on with them and their relationship burned in her head, but she couldn't ask with Ben's mind so occupied with his gram.

Maybe tonight when they got home.

Chapter Twenty-Three

Gram never stabilized that evening, and Ben ended up staying at the hospital. He'd sent Riley home with Cassidy. He and his half brothers stayed. It made the room crowded, but Gram had been instrumental in all of their lives, and none of them wanted to walk away from her at this critical time. He'd called the twins, and they were coming down.

Tough was still and quiet in the corner. Turbo paced. Torque and Ben sat in chairs on either side of the bed. None of them needed to say much. Either she'd live or she'd die. Either way, they were here for her. It's all they could do.

Ben spent a lot of that long night thinking about Riley and the chances he'd let slip away. Maybe he should have fought harder for her. Maybe he was too consumed with the twins and raising them. Maybe he'd allowed his hurt over her first rejection to keep him from pursuing her again.

Whatever it was, whatever he could have done differently, he couldn't change it. He could have regrets and wallow in that misery, or he could let it all go and start fresh.

The nurse had just left after taking Gram's vitals, and the clock said 2 a.m.

Ben spoke in the stillness of the room. "Riley and I just got married this spring. It was basically a marriage of convenience because she needed me at the shop and because I needed a wife or I would have to admit to Gram that I lied about being married for years."

"Huh?" Turbo stopped pacing and stared at Ben.

"Then you fell in love with her," Torque said, ignoring Turbo.

"She fell in love with you." Tough spoke from the corner where he stood with his arms and one leg crossed.

They all stared at him.

"Did you tell her?" Tough asked.

"Tell her what?" Turbo asked.

"Just this evening," Ben said, ignoring Turbo.

"Maybe you two ought to take off work and go on a honeymoon," Torque said.

"You just suggested he take off work?" Turbo asked incredulously.

"Wait until Gram stabilizes," Tough said, ignoring Turbo.

"Would you guys quit acting like I'm not here," Turbo said.

"Don't wait on me," Gram said, ignoring Turbo. "Not everyone gets even one chance at a lifetime love. It's not something to take for granted."

Everyone looked at her in surprise. They hadn't realized she was awake. Tough and Turbo moved to the foot of her bed. Torque stood up and leaned over. "Are you feeling better?"

"I shouldn't have tried to change the sheets on my bed. I think I pulled a muscle in my chest." She tapped her chest.

Ben blinked at Gram. "You were changing sheets?"

"That's why we've been staying with you. So that you don't have to do stuff like that." Torque covered Gram's frail hand with his own.

Gram's tired eyes swept over Ben's face. "I think they're going to yell at me some. You go home and talk to your new wife. I think you have some things to work out."

Ben leaned over and kissed Gram's cool cheek. "Thanks, Gram."

"Hey," Turbo said. "Your woman left and took your wheels."

Ben's chest caved. He'd forgotten. He'd have to ask her to come back and get him, and he couldn't do that at 2 a.m.

Turbo tossed him keys. "Take mine."

Ben snatched them out of the air. "Thanks, bro."

～

RILEY COULDN'T SLEEP. She should have stayed at the hospital. Worry about Gram was some of it, but thinking about Ben, and what he'd said at the restaurant, and how they were going to work things out kept spinning around in her head.

Finally, she wrapped a blanket around herself and padded down to the porch. It would be several hours before the sun came up, but she felt closer to Ben, and with the uncertainty rolling around in her chest, it eased her mind to sit where they'd spent so many peaceful mornings.

She'd only been outside for thirty minutes when his truck came up the drive.

It took her a few seconds to realize that it wasn't Ben's truck since she'd driven his truck home. Hoping it was one of his brothers dropping him off, and wondering what that meant for Gram, she waited, holding her breath.

The driver's door opened. A short pang went through her until she recognized the broad shoulders and confident walk as Ben strode up to the porch.

"How is she?" Riley asked.

Ben stopped, his gaze searching the porch shadows. "Gram's fine. What's the matter?"

She stood. "Couldn't sleep."

He found her and walked toward her. "I'm glad you're up. I need you to know I meant every word I said tonight." His hands landed on her hips through the blanket.

"I was hoping you did." She swallowed. "I did too. Whatever is going on between us is more important to me than anything that's happening with my dad or the company."

He sighed. "I don't want you to have to choose."

"That's more considerate than him." She pulled her hand out of the blanket, holding her phone. She pressed the button so he could read the text message her dad had sent while they were in the hospital.

160

> I'll give you 50% of the company and the
> corner office I promised you if you lose the
> mechanic.

Ben read it, and his hands dropped. He turned. She let the blanket fall to the floor along with her phone and wrapped her arms around him, resting her head on his back.

"That's everything you've always wanted, right there," he said, bitterness seeping into his voice.

"It's not."

"You can say that," he said roughly. "But we both know it's a lie."

"It's not!" She let go of him, moving to the side. "I've spent the last twenty years of my life regretting the night I stood you up for prom. I insulted you. I lied to you. And I have no right to get a second chance with you. I've worked hard to try to make sure it wasn't the worst decision I ever made, but it was. The *very* worst decision I ever made. If there's any good thing that can come from that, it's that I'm never going to make an awful decision like that again. Ever."

Ben wouldn't look at her. He stared off into the night, his arms crossed over his chest.

She put both hands on her cheeks. "Ben, please. I'm sorry. I'm so very sorry. Let me have some time to make it up to you."

"It's not about making anything up to me. Just having you beside me is enough." He looked down at her. "Your arms around me, your smile in the morning, your name with mine...it's enough."

Her heart hammered. Was he saying what she thought he was saying? Her words came out hesitantly. "You want to stay married?"

His hands came up, gripping her shoulders. "I want to be married. For real. Forever."

"Me too."

He kissed her then, on the porch where they'd watched so many new days dawn, and it felt like a new day dawning in her own life as she clung to him, kissing him back with all her heart.

Chapter Twenty-Four

"Ben?"

His eyes didn't want to open, and he didn't want to untangle himself from the soft body next to him, but years of raising kids had him answering, "What do you need, Eve?"

The door squeaked. Then Eve squeaked. "Oh, my goodness! That's a sight I've never seen before. Eden, come quick!"

Which is what his wife woke up to—his sister standing in his open door, gawking at him still in bed at nine in the morning. "First day of work I've missed in your entire lives, and I can't even sleep in."

"What is it?" Eden's voice came from the stairs.

"Ben's in bed with a woman!"

Eden appeared beside Eve in the doorway.

"That's not just any woman. It's Riley."

"I know. It's just...the first time this has ever happened."

Beside him, Riley stirred. Her arm was slung over his chest, and her leg was bent over his. Her head lay on his shoulder, and the confident scent of her filled his mind.

"I'm married to her. This is what married people do."

"Very funny, Ben. You've been married to her for five months, and married people weren't doing that then."

Riley moved her head, putting her lips on his neck. He closed his eyes. "Those are *your* kids, right?"

The twins laughed. "We're sorry, Riley. We had to rib Ben. It's almost unheard of for us to see him in bed, morning or night, and he's never had a girl."

"I've never been married before."

Riley stretched under the covers. "You girls can go cook us lunch."

"What about breakfast?"

They smiled at each other. "We're skipping it."

The twins backed out and shut the door.

Ben turned on his side and ran his finger down Riley's cheek. "I think you're glowing, wife."

She laughed. "I feel like I'm glowing. You look kinda happy yourself."

"I'm happy. Beyond words. But I'm a little nervous you might regret picking me."

"I have a little experience in the transportation industry. Maybe together we can make something out of ourselves."

Ben's finger traced the delicate line of her jaw. "That would be a huge conflict of interest. You can't help me start a repair shop if you're still in your dad's business."

"He texted me this morning with an ultimatum. 'Leave the mechanic or quit.' I told him where the reports were and asked him if he wanted me to work out a two-week notice."

"Only half of me is happy about that."

"I think Dad will come around. What good's a company when you're all alone?"

"That's a good question."

"Plus the investors were pretty clear they wanted you. I think Dad's bluffing. But I don't care if he is. It won't change my mind."

Ben leaned down and kissed her forehead. "Does that mean we're going to do this together?"

"I'd love to. Someone around here has said that we make a good team." Her teeth flashed, and he pulled her closer. "I've also heard that you are an excellent father."

A little shot of surprise constricted his throat. "I guess I kind of figured you were a no-kids kind of girl."

She bit her lip. "We could team up with that, too."

"Gotta say, it'd be nice to have a partner."

"In everything."

"Are we setting up this partnership in Maine?"

"Pennsylvania," she said with assurance.

It's what he wanted too. After all, he had a reason to be here now. "So, my wife is going to bring me back to my family?"

"I'm going to make sure you stay where you belong."

"Where's that?"

"With me."

He kissed her then and wouldn't have stopped for a long time, but his phone rang.

"Gram?" Riley lifted a brow.

He reluctantly reached for it, turning it on speaker. "Hello?" He figured he probably sounded like he was lying in bed with his wife. First time in his life he sounded like that. He smiled.

"Someone told me you got fired," Torque said by way of greeting.

"Word gets around." Technically he hadn't gotten fired. Not yet. But he wasn't at work, so people would naturally make that assumption. Not to mention he'd never given a thought to who else might have been in the restaurant yesterday.

"Yeah. Would you and Riley be interested in coming to my shop today, taking my customers and watching our kids? Dusty is making a run for the championship, and Cassidy decided this morning she wanted to go."

Ben lifted his brows at Riley.

She nodded. "We'll do it."

"Great. How soon can you two be out of bed and over here?"

They smiled at each other. "I guess we're just not destined to lie around together."

"We have the rest of our lives."

~

Join Jessie's list and be the first to know about new releases and sales on her books!

<u>Read For Keep with You</u>, the next book in the Baxter Boys series where Dusty has an accident and works to get back on the track. Her therapist is the best, and he's also the one man who has ever caught her interest. Keep reading for a sneak peek now.

Sneak Peek of For Keeps With You

Dusty Gibson focused her eyes on the black number two before slamming the visor of her helmet down. The noise of the other competitors faded out, making her feel like she had entered an alternate reality.

Her bike rumbled beneath her.

The two changed to a one.

She flicked her wrist, twisting the handle and pumping the gas. With her other hand she squeezed the clutch. Her bike trembled in eager anticipation.

The one turned sideways.

Two seconds later the gates fell. Dusty dropped the clutch and twisted her wrist. Engines screamed around her. Grabbing the clutch, she jerked her foot, caught second and sprang ahead. A guy in purple on her left edged closer. On her right a yellow jersey and a red jersey fought for position.

She jammed third, then fourth gear, keeping her eyes on the first jump. Ideal position would be the leader of the pack at that point. She hadn't gotten to be the points leader in motocross racing by running in the back.

Running wide open she angled to the left, toward purple shirt who was running even with her. From her practice runs, she knew the direct middle of the jump had a slight dip that, hit the wrong way, could cause her bike to flip end over end. Not what she wanted to have happen with a whole class of fifteen aggressive racers behind her.

Purple shirt gave the space, then pushed back. Dusty jerked to avoid smacking his foot peg.

Her bike caught, her handle bars twisted. She jerked them back, keeping the throttle on wide open. Sweat trickled down her forehead. The visor on her helmet steamed up, fogging her vision. She could see the horizon where blue met brown, but couldn't judge the distance to the first jump. Fifty feet? Thirty?

She needed to get out of the middle. Pushing again at purple shirt, she refused to allow anything but cool determination to sit in her chest. She'd done this a thousand times before. But purple shirt either didn't see her or was determined to keep her boxed in.

The latter was quite possible, since she was the current points leader and, hence, the person to beat.

Her bike screamed beneath her. She twisted hard on the throttle, keeping it wide open. She wanted to catch a big lift on that jump. But not from the middle.

Changing up, she pushed against yellow shirt on her right. But red shirt ran tire to tire with him and he couldn't give her the space if he wanted to.

She tried purple shirt again. Still no budging.

In a split second her three options ran through her brain: force purple shirt to move, with contact, if necessary, risking a crash for both of them; slow down, let him and red and yellow go by, which was surely the plan of the other three leaders; or shift her weight off her front tire and hit the jump flat in the middle. The third option would have been the only one she would have considered, except she couldn't see.

She hadn't expected it to be this hot and she hadn't put her anti-fog on her visor. Rookie mistake.

A decision had to be made. Fast.

Pushing once more at purple shirt, who didn't budge from her side, she crouched on her pegs and squinted, wanting to get the timing just right. Pulling up would slow her down. Not much, but enough to let the others get ahead. Where she wanted to be. Where she was going to be. Nothing was going to stop her from becoming the first female motocross champion.

Suddenly the jump loomed up in front of her, faster than she had estimated. She stood and leaned back, but she was a millisecond too late.

Her front tire dipped. Her body hitched forward. Her biked kicked up, and she was flung over the handle bars, spread-eagle in the air. Purple shirt had decided at the last minute to move over, giving way to a guy in a blue shirt. She caught it out of the corner of her eye in the split second she hung upside down and backward in the air.

The split second before he crashed into her.

A crack sounded loud in her ears. Pain flared up her back and out both arms. Her body flung wildly.

She saw the next bike coming and tried to twist, but the pain radiated out in sharp spikes, and her mind went black.

~

Four weeks later

"This one's yours." Sherri, the office nurse, handed Roland Bryant a folder with a smirk. The harsh florescent lighting in their physical therapy office glanced off the pristine white walls with tasteful overblown photos of palm trees hung in an even spread.

He took the folder as he stood behind the high counter and opened it.

Sherri put one hand on the counter. Her bright red nails sparkled. "They requested 'the best.'" She laughed. "You know what that means." With a lifting of her brows she walked away.

Roland swallowed his snort. When a client requested "the best" it was almost always because they were "the worst." Not the worst as in the physical worse, but the worse as in the most difficult to deal with. He always got those.

His eyes skimmed over the folder. The client would be waiting in the big room where all the therapy sessions were held, but he always liked a little privacy to familiarize himself with a new patient's background before he met them. Some injuries were so horrific he couldn't contain his grimace. Some were unusual, requiring him to do a quick search or even shoot off a few emails to colleagues, for their advice and opinion on best practices.

Dusty Gibson. Twenty-six. He'd fractured his femur and vertebrae T-11 and T-12 in a motocross race. Roland shuddered. There was a starred note that he was a top contender, and insisted that he would race again.

Maybe Roland was "the best" but he wasn't a miracle worker and Dusty was flipping lucky he wasn't paralyzed.

Yeah. He closed the folder, already picturing in his head exercises that would strengthen the rarely used muscles in the back that would help Dusty until his leg was fully healed.

Normally, Roland worked the best with the patients who were discouraged, who needed someone with a story of their own to breathe hope back into a client who wondered what their life was going to consist of now that they were no longer perfectly whole. That, Roland could do. He just told his own story. Leaving his dead fiancée out of it.

With a last glance to make sure all the proper forms had been signed, he carried the folder out. He glanced inconspicuously around the room. Dusty wouldn't be the older gentleman, nor the three senior ladies scattered through the room. A skinny elementary school aged boy sat beside a woman, his mother presumably, with his arm in a brace and his ball cap pulled down over his forehead.

Roland's eyes skimmed over all of those. Dusty would have a leg brace; he might even be in a wheelchair. Only two people in the patient waiting corner of the large room could possibly be twenty-eight years old. A man who did not have a leg cast and a slim woman with waist-length blond hair who did.

She also wore a backbrace.

Dusty Gibson, motocross champion, was a woman.

Roland dealt with men, women, boys, girls, old men and senior ladies. So the odd reaction of his heart, which twisted in his chest, was unexpected. And unwelcome.

He put his game face on. "Dusty Gibson."

The blond rose stiffly, which is the only way one could move in a back brace. She turned. Roland's heart twisted again. Harder. Her wide blue eyes turned in his direction, looking for the source of the summons. A heart-shaped face, cute nose, and high cheekbones complimented that long, straight hair. Her carriage was proud and despite the braces, she moved with a cat-like grace.

No wheelchair. She wasn't even using crutches. He obviously hadn't studied her chart in enough depth.

He pointed to the first counseling room along the side. "We're going there. Let me grab your chart." It wasn't the way he normally met patients, but Dusty had already turned his "normal" upside down and he hadn't even introduced himself yet.

In the course of his practice as a physical therapist, he'd had a few patients that had stuck with him, either because of the severity of their injuries, their amazing personalities or because of their grit and determination. He knew for sure Dusty was going to be one of those patients he didn't forget.

Grabbing her chart, he caught up to her in time to open the counseling room door for her. She gave him a disdainful look. "I can get it myself."

"I'm sure you can."

"Don't patronize me."

She wasn't the first person who came in for therapy with a bad attitude. Now wasn't the time for tough love. That would come soon enough. "I'm sorry," he said.

She walked through the door without another word. He followed, closing it behind him.

Dusty wanted to fling herself down in the light blue plastic seat, but her back and leg both still hurt and she wasn't going to fling herself anywhere for a while. So she sat. Gingerly. Hating the fact that her once agile and strong body was crippled and painful.

It wasn't the therapist's fault, though. "I'm sorry I snapped at you," she said, grudgingly as the man dressed in khaki pants and a blue polo with the logo of the therapy place in white letters on his shirt stopped in front of her.

"It's okay. I know this isn't where you want to be."

She snorted. "Not even close."

"So that's my job. To get you better so you don't have to come here anymore."

The guy was affable and not bad-looking. She gave him a half-smile. "Let's get started."

"I think that's my line."

"You gotta be fast if you want to beat me."

"Let's start at the beginning, then." He held out his hand. "I'm Roland, and I'm going to be coordinating your therapy for the next six months or so."

She smirked, grabbing his proffered hand. "I'm Dusty, and I'm going to do one month, maybe six weeks of this crap, then I'm going back on the circuit." She met his eyes while she spoke. Deep and solid green, they seemed to be searching straight into her soul. Something about his expression, his firm, warm handshake, his confident bearing – she wasn't sure what it was, but she trusted him immediately, which was unusual for her. Usually people had to prove themselves to her.

He blinked, pulling his hand away. Instead of walking around and sitting on the other side of the desk that took up most of the small room, he perched on the corner of it, on her side.

"Are you comfortable in that chair?" he asked.

"Not really."

He jerked his head at the chair behind the desk. "Sit there. It'll be a lot easier on your back and leg."

She didn't appreciate the command given without even a modification in the way of a "please." But in her current state, it was hard to get comfortable, and she'd take what she could get.

"Thank you," she said, standing carefully. He made no move to help her. Not that she could blame him after she about snapped his head off when he opened the door for her. She gimped around and sat in the big, comfortable office chair.

"There's a stool there to prop your leg on."

She looked down, and sure enough, a small, wooden stool poked out from under the desk. "Thanks."

His head was bent over her chart. "You're welcome," he said without lifting his head.

She could tell him what was in the chart. That's she'd fractured two vertebrae and her femur. Torn ligaments in her knee and right shoulder. Bruised five ribs. Was lucky to be walking.

Whatever. The season was going on without her, and she wanted to get back out. She had been so close to being the first woman to ever win the big championship. She hated feeling that slip through her fingers. Technically, so far she'd only missed three points races. Even though she hadn't raced, she was still fifth in the standings. She could still pull off a win. And how much sweeter it would be winning after coming back from such a massive setback.

The seconds ticked away. Dusty resisted the urge to squirm. She wasn't used to sitting still this long.

When he finally looked up, he didn't ask any of the questions she'd been expecting. "Where's your ride?"

She rolled her eyes. It was written right in her chart that she wasn't allowed to drive. "My friend dropped me off. She had some errands to run and a baby and toddler that will fare much better at the park down the road than in the waiting room here."

"I'd like to meet her when she picks you up."

She glared at him. "That's your way of making sure I didn't ride my Harley here?"

His eyes brows lifted a fraction. *Ha.*

"I hadn't considered that you might ride your Harley to your first outpatient physical therapy session after breaking your back, your femur, bruising your ribs, and ripping ligaments in your knee and shoulder." He tilted his head. "My bad."

She snorted, trying to keep her lips from quirking up. "It's easy to underestimate me."

"I'll keep that in mind." He tapped the chart. "I see you just got permission today to walk on that leg. It's only been four weeks. Did you have the doctor in a headlock when he wrote that?"

She pursed her lips. "No." She waited a beat. "I had him pinned to the floor with his arm twisted back and up around his ear." Crossing her arms over her chest she waited.

He nodded like she'd told him the truth. "Another thing to keep in mind."

Her eyes ran over his torso and noted how his biceps strained against the sleeves of his polo shirt. She wasn't going to man handle him. Not that she was used to winning in physical contests. Soaking wet she might weight one hundred ten pounds. No, if she wanted to beat the boys, she had to do it on her bike.

And right now, she needed this guy to help her. "Listen, the doc at my appointment today didn't really want me walking without the crutches. But my femur wasn't a compound fracture, it was just a crack, and the x-rays clearly show that a good solid bit of bone has formed over the split. The best thing I can do for it is to start using it regularly."

His lips thinned, but he didn't argue with her. She appreciated that quality in a man.

"Well, you definitely surprised me when you're only four weeks out and don't have crutches." He crossed his arms over his chest. His shirt stretched tight. Dusty kept her eyes pointed up at his face. "A wheelchair wouldn't have surprised me." He wiggled the folder that was under his arm. "I definitely knew I needed to go back and read your chart in detail." His jaw stuck out. "Some clients I have to motivate to move, and some I have to hold back. I know what category you belong to."

"Me too. And you're not holding me back. There's a big race in six weeks and I'm planning on being in it."

His mouth tightened and his eyes slid away, but, again, he didn't argue. Good.

"You've got to understand, Dusty, that doing too much can be just as detrimental as not doing enough. I'm on board to get you up and moving like you're used to, without pain, as fast as we can. I'll work with you as hard as I can. But in return, you've got to promise me that you're not going to jeopardize our progress by pushing farther than I say you can."

He raised his brow. She dropped her eyes. Everything in her was on "go fast." She didn't really have another speed. But again, that feeling that she could trust him, sat like a comforting hand on her shoulder.

"Dusty, you broke your back. You're very lucky we're talking about getting back normal motion instead of me teaching you how to empty your catheter bag."

She jerked her head. "It didn't happen and we're not talking about it."

"I think you can regain full motor function, and I think you can live pain-free for the most part. But only if you do this right. You've got great reports from your surgeries and from the hospital therapists. Let's do this thing right, Dusty."

She found herself nodding before she even realized it. "Okay. I'll do what you say."

"That's the attitude." He stood. "Let's go out and get started."

Sign up for Jessie's newsletter! Get a free book, access to exclusive bonus content, get fun and funny updates on her life on the farm and more!

A Gift from Jessie

View this code through your smart phone camera to be taken to a page where you can download a FREE ebook when you sign up to get updates from Jessie Gussman! Find out why people say, "Jessie's is the only newsletter I open and read" and "You make my day brighter. Love, love, love reading your newsletters. I don't know where you find time to write books. You are so busy living life. A true blessing." and "I know from now on that I can't be drinking my morning coffee while reading your newsletter – I laughed so hard I sprayed it out all over the table!"

Claim your free book from Jessie!

Escape to more faith-filled romance series by Jessie Gussman!

The Complete Sweet Water, North Dakota Reading Order:

Series One: Sweet Water Ranch Western Cowboy Romance (11 book series)

Series Two: Coming Home to North Dakota (12 book series)

Series Three: Flyboys of Sweet Briar Ranch in North Dakota (13 book series)

Series Four: Sweet View Ranch Western Cowboy Romance (10 book series)

Spinoffs and More! Additional Series You'll Love:

Jessie's First Series: Sweet Haven Farm (4 book series)

Small-Town Romance: The Baxter Boys (5 book series)

Bad-Boy Sweet Romance: Richmond Rebels Sweet Romance (3 book series)

Sweet Water Spinoff: Cowboy Crossing (9 book series)

Small Town Romantic Comedy: Good Grief, Idaho (5 book series)

True Stories from Jessie's Farm: Stories from Jessie Gussman's Newsletter (3 book series)

Reader-Favorite! Sweet Beach Romance: Blueberry Beach (8 book series)

Blueberry Beach Spinoff: Strawberry Sands (10 book series)

From Strawberry Sands to: Raspberry Ridge (12 book series)

Swoonfully Jolly Holiday Stories:

Holiday Romance: Cowboy Mountain Christmas (6 book series)

Cowboy Mountain Christmas Spinoff: A Heartland Cowboy Christmas (9 book series)

New and Much Loved: Mistletoe Meadows (4 books and counting!)

Laughing Through the Snow: Christmas Tree, PA Sweet Romcoms (6 short reads)